Harlequin
Presents..

Other titles by

ANNE MATHER
IN HARLEQUIN PRESENTS

#17 LIVING WITH ADAM _____ 75c
#20 A DISTANT SOUND OF THUNDER ___ 75c
#23 THE LEGEND OF LEXANDROS _____ 75c
#26 DARK ENEMY _____ 75c
#29 MONKSHOOD _____ 75c
#32 JAKE HOWARD'S WIFE _____ 75c
#35 SEEN BY CANDLELIGHT _____ 75c
#38 MOON WITCH _____ 75c
#41 DANGEROUS ENCHANTMENT _____ 75c
#46 PRELUDE TO ENCHANTMENT _____ 75c
#49 A SAVAGE BEAUTY _____ 75c
#54 THE NIGHT OF THE BULLS _____ 75c
#57 LEGACY OF THE PAST _____ 75c
#61 CHASE A GREEN SHADOW _____ 75c
#65 WHITE ROSE OF WINTER _____ 75c
#69 MASTER OF FALCON'S HEAD _____ 75c
#74 LEOPARD IN THE SNOW _____ 75c
#77 THE JAPANESE SCREEN _____ 75c
#86 RACHEL TREVELLYAN _____ 95c
#92 MASK OF SCARS _____ 95c
#96 SILVER FRUIT UPON SILVER TREES _ 95c
#100 DARK MOONLESS NIGHT _____ 95c

ANNE MATHER

no gentle possession

HARLEQUIN BOOKS
toronto-winnipeg

Harlequin Presents edition published August 1975
SBN 373-70605-7

Original hard cover edition published in 1973
by Mills & Boon Limited

Printed in Canada.

CHAPTER ONE

THE long room with its pine-logged walls and low-beamed ceiling was full of people, most of whom were stamping their feet and clapping excitedly to the sound of Tyrolean music gone slightly mad. The small band of local musicians had all imbibed rather freely of their host's hospitality, as indeed had everyone else, and by now the party was totally uninhibited, dancing and singing, or keeping time with their feet. At the far end of the room a huge fireplace was filled with logs which blazed brightly, adding their own illumination to the scene, while the atmosphere, thickened by cigar and cigarette smoke, exuded the mingled scents of perfume and shaving lotion, wines and lager, or plain body heat.

At the opposite end of the room to the fire, a man sat apart from the rest, lodged on a tall stool beside the long buffet tables where food and drink were being dispensed by several white-coated attendants. For time to time, someone would approach him with the obvious idea of rousing him from his solitude, but from their expressions when they turned away it was just as obvious that they had not succeeded.

Alexis Whitney was bored. It was no new experience for him. He was often bored, more frequently with people than with places, and right now he was in no mood to appreciate the kind of *bonhomie* that was created at such a gathering. He was well aware that his attitude would have been noted and commented upon; it wasn't very kind, it wasn't even very polite, but quite honestly he didn't particularly care. He was all too compellingly aware that no matter how rude or objectionable he might be, his so-called friends would forgive him, and if that forgiveness was conceived all the more rapidly

5

because of his father's undoubted wealth and social position, then who was he to complain? It was a cynical attitude, he knew, but events had generated that cynicism, and looking ahead he could see no reason to change his opinions.

Finishing the remaining Scotch in his glass, he rose to his feet, flexing his back muscles tiredly. He had spent the day on the ski slopes above the village and although during the past couple of weeks he had done a lot of skiing, today he had really taxed his strength and endurance. It had been another attempt to shed the boredom that seemed to be seeping like a poison into his soul.

His amber eyes surveyed the room critically. There must have been about forty people present, almost all the guests from the Grüssmatte Hotel, in fact. But Axel Fritzlander was like that. He threw open his chalet without reserve, inviting anyone and everyone to his parties. Alexis had known him for about twenty years. He was a contemporary of his father's, and Alexis could remember coming here years ago when he was only a child and his mother had been alive. They had spent many winter holidays at the Grüssmatte Hotel, and in consequence they knew its owner intimately. Now, of course, Grüssmatte was much busier than it had been then, and there were other small hotels and *pensions* catering for the ever-increasing influx of tourists, but still the hotel owned by Axel Fritzlander maintained its individuality, and his guests expected and received personal service. It was expensive, of course, much more expensive than the Hochlander, or the Gasthof, but that, said Axel, was the only way to ensure that his guests would be of the right type and background to mix socially. To Alexis, in his present frame of mind, it was all rather pretentious, and he half wished he had chosen to stay at one of the other hotels, just to see what kind of a reaction that would have aroused.

Still, he thought reflectively, these weeks in Austria

6

had served their purpose in that they had taken him away from London at a time when he most desired it. He had come to the Grüssmatte with David Vanning, a young barrister in London, and one of his few real friends. They had gone to school together, but nowadays, since David began his career, they didn't see much of one another. Alexis recalled with wry humour his father's astonishment when he had told him he was going away with David. The usual crowd he mixed with didn't go in much for actual working, and until recently he had been quite happy to go along with their philosophy so long as he remained conscious of his father's displeasure . . .

At the moment, David was at the opposite end of the room, sitting near the fire with Rosemary Lawson, whose parents had not joined the party. Rosemary had been David's prime objective in coming to the Grüssmatte, he had made that clear from the start, but Alexis had not minded. It had suited him to have some time alone; it had given him a chance to think, and while he didn't particularly care for his thoughts, at least he had enjoyed the sense of release gained in purely physical achievement.

Now he made his way towards the door, but before he reached it, a small, slim, red-haired girl interposed herself between him and his goal.

'Alex darling,' she exclaimed appealingly, grasping the sleeve of his dark blue suede suit. 'You're not leaving!'

Alexis looked down at her wryly. 'Aren't I? I thought I was.'

'Oh, Alex, you can't go now! It's only just after midnight! Darling, why aren't you joining in the fun like everybody else? It's not like you to be so – so – detached!'

Alexis shrugged. 'I'm sorry,' he said. But it was a refusal.

The girl's hand dropped from his sleeve. She had to tip back her head to look up at him. 'What's the matter?

What have I done? You've scarcely spoken to me for the last five days!' Her voice quivered a little. 'I thought – I thought you liked me.'

Alexis controlled his impatience. He despised women who ran after a man, who could not control their emotions. 'I do like you, Sara,' he replied briefly. 'But right now I'm tired, I want to go to bed.'

Sara Raymond touched a strand of her hair provocatively. 'I don't mind where you want to go, if I can go with you.'

Alexis expelled his breath on a long sigh. 'No, Sara,' he said definitely, and with a faint smile he walked past her to the door.

No one else tried to stop him. Only Axel was likely to have attempted to do so, and he was occupied with a group of people near the band. Alexis cast one last look at the scene, and then went out into the hall.

He collected his sheepskin coat, and fastened it warmly before stepping out into the frosty air. He scorned the fur hats worn by some and his hair, which at first sight could appear almost white because of its silvery lightness, lay thick and smooth against his head. It was a magnificent night, the sky an arc of inky blue above, inset with a million jewel-like stars. All around the chalet, and the village on whose outskirts it lay, the mountains slumbered beneath their pall of snow like rampant giants, their startling whiteness illuminating the scene with brilliant clarity.

Hunching his shoulders, Alexis set off to walk back to the hotel, but as it was only some hundred yards from Axel's chalet, he decided to walk the length of the village before retiring. Now that he was away from the party, from the thick, cloying atmosphere, his brain felt sharper, and clearer, and the weariness in his bones seemed to ease as he moved.

There were still one or two people about, although most were enjoying the kind of *après-ski* entertainment

Axel provided, and the sound of accordion music drifted on the air. But it was not an unpleasant sound, and Alexis felt more at peace with himself at that moment than at any time he could recently remember.

It did not take long to reach the end of the village where the bare iron supports of the ski-lift stood out starkly against the background of snow. Motionless now, they stretched up towards the line of spruce and pine trees which marked the beginning of the higher slopes. During the day, these lower slopes were thronged with people, young and old alike, but the more rarefied atmosphere of the upper slopes was what Alexis preferred.

He was about to turn back again when a movement some way up the slope caught his attention. Someone was up there, and because they were wearing something light, they had not immediately been noticeable. Alexis frowned. Surely no one was foolhardy enough to be messing about at this time of night without anyone on hand to offer assistance should it be necessary. Even these lower slopes could be treacherous, providing their users with twisted ankles, sprained muscles, and sometimes actual broken limbs.

He hesitated. It was really nothing to do with him. If his eyes were not so accustomed to searching the slopes for possible dangers on his own perilous descents he might never have noticed that there was anyone up there.

But even as he considered this, there was a startled cry and the person, whoever it was, overbalanced and came tumbling down the slope towards him. It was obvious in that undignified descent that whoever it was was not wearing skis, and Alexis gave a resigned sigh before he went to help the unfortunate climber out of the drift of snow into which he had tumbled.

However, as he reached the place where the snow was thickest, the climber was scrambling to his feet, and brushing himself down, so that clearly there was no damage done. Alexis halted, and then said:

9

'Are you all right?'

The climber started, as though until that moment he had thought himself alone, but as he looked up Alexis saw that his supposition of which sex had been wrong. It was a girl who stood regarding him with obvious impatience, a tall girl with an oval face, unnaturally pale in the moonlight, and dark, very dark hair that strayed in a deep fringe across her forehead, and pushed out from the bottom of the cream fur hood of the parka she was wearing.

She stared at him for a moment, her eyes narrowing so that he could scarcely see them between the thick lashes, and then dropping her gaze she said: 'I'm perfectly all right, thank you,' dispelling any doubts he might have had as to her nationality. Her voice was low and attractive, and unmistakably English.

Alexis inclined his head. 'That's good.' He paused. 'However, I wouldn't advise you to do this very often. These slopes have been known to produce quite serious accidents, and as you're not even wearing skis . . .'

She looked up then, anger quickening her speech. 'I'm quite aware of the hazards involved, thank you.'

'Are you?' his expression was wry. 'Is that why you made that ungainly descent from up there?' His eyes flickered up towards the firs. 'I'm sorry – it's something quite new to me. I always thought the idea was to remain in an upright position. Obviously, I was wrong—'

'Very amusing!' She made an irritated little grimace at him and giving one last flick to her cream trousers began to walk towards the village.

Alexis smiled, watching her retreating back with humour. Then with a characteristic shrug of his broad shoulders he quickened his stride to fall into step beside her. 'I'm sorry,' he said, with that innate charm which was so much a part of his attractiveness. 'But I couldn't resist it. You looked so indignant standing there, all covered in snow. It's a pity I was around at all.'

'Yes, it was.'

The girl looked at him out of the corners of her eyes, and something stirred way back in his subconscious. Something about her was vaguely familiar; he had the disturbing suspicion that at some time she had looked at him like that before. But how was it possible? It was obvious from her accent that she was not from the southern part of England, nor did she have the cultured overtones in her voice that he was used to. How could he have met someone like her? Unless it was at university . . .

He frowned. It was an infuriating impression, and on impulse, he said: 'Have we ever met before?'

Immediately the words were out he regretted using them. She lifted her dark eyebrows mockingly, and replied: 'Is that the best you can do? I expected something quite devastating after that introduction!'

Alexis's frowned deepened. He didn't like being made to feel small. 'It was not a line,' he said. 'I meant it.'

'Really?' She sounded uninterested, and a slow feeling of anger began to burn inside him. It was a long time since any woman had treated him to such a show of indifference, and he resented her assumption that he might be interested in her.

In cool tones, he said: 'I should have realized it was impossible to ask such a question without you assuming I was necessarily voicing a personal interest in you. I'm sorry if I'm exploding the high opinion you have of yourself, but there it is.'

The girl tensed at this, and for a moment he felt contrite. He felt quite sure that could he have seen her in normal lighting and not the eerie artificiality of the moon he would have found her cheeks to be blazing with colour at the intended slight.

But she made no reply and not really knowing what prompted him to do so, Alexis said: 'Are you staying long in Grüssmatte?'

There was a moment's silence while she obviously fought with herself as to whether to reply, and then she said: 'Actually no. We leave in the morning.'

'I see.' Alexis thrust his hands deep into the pockets of his sheepskin coat. 'Will you be sorry to leave?'

'Not really,' she conceded quietly. 'I – well – two other teachers and myself are responsible for thirty teenagers. It hasn't exactly been a picnic.'

Alexis was interested in spite of himself, but at that moment she halted and gestured towards the small hotel standing back from the road. 'We're staying here,' she said. 'Good night.'

Alexis's brows drew together. All of a sudden he wished they had not had that altercation. He would have liked to have continued talking to her. But she was already walking up the slope towards the hotel and short of going after her and risking another rebuff there was nothing he could do. And he still had that annoying sensation that he had met her before.

He arrived back at the Grüssmatte Hotel, not in the best of tempers, and when the hotel manager stopped him in the hall with a tentative: 'Herr Whitney!' he turned to him with ill-concealed impatience.

'Yes? What is it?'

Jurgen Blass gave an apologetic smile. 'So sorry to trouble you, Herr Whitney, but there has been a telephone call for you – from your father.'

Alexis sighed. 'Yes?'

'He – er – would like you to ring him back as soon as you come in, Herr Whitney. He said it was urgent.'

'Urgent? At this time of night?' Alexis glanced at the gold watch on his wrist.

'Yes, Herr Whitney.'

Alexis considered the man's impassive face for a moment and then shrugged. 'Very well. Arrange the call for me, will you? I'll be in my suite.'

'Yes, sir.'

The manager bowed his head politely and Alexis went on his way to the stairs. For all its excellence, the Grüssmatte had no lifts.

While he waited for the call to come through, Alexis took a shower. It was when he was towelling himself dry that the telephone in the adjoining bedroom began to ring. Wrapping the huge towel around him, he went to answer it. Until that moment he had not paid a great deal of attention as to why his father should want to speak to him at this time of night, his thoughts had still been absorbed with the girl from the ski slopes, but now as he lifted the receiver recollections of his life in London came back to him, and he felt a sense of resentment that because of this medium there was no real escape.

'Alexis Whitney,' he responded automatically.

'Alex! Alex – is that you?' His father's voice was indistinct. It was not a good line.

'Yes, Howard. Where's the fire?' He was laconic. It was a long time since he and his father had had any real communication with one another. They saw one another frequently, they talked frequently; but always there was that unseen barrier between them.

'Alex! I've been trying to reach you since ten o'clock!'

'I was out.'

'I know that, dammit. Couldn't you leave notification as to where you are?'

'They knew where I was.'

'Then why the hell didn't somebody contact you?'

'I guess you didn't make the position too clear.' Alexis was bored with this conversation. 'In any case, I don't see why whatever you've got to say couldn't wait until morning.'

'Don't you? Don't you?' Howard Whitney was breathing heavily down the telephone and Alexis could picture him propped against the desk in his study, his face reddening with frustration as he endeavoured to restrain the temper which Alexis himself had inherited. A big man, as tall as Alexis himself but stockily built with a thickening waistline, he was forced to maintain a rigid diet to avoid the blood pressure which was already evident in times of stress. 'Damn you, Alex, do you know what Knight has done? He's attempted suicide!'

'What?' Alexis, who had been reaching for one of the slim cigars he favoured, stayed his hand. 'You mean – he's dead!'

'No.' His father bit off the word harshly. 'No, fortunately he was found in time. He's not dead – just off his head, I hear.'

Alexis took a deep breath and wrapped the towel more closely about him. 'I see.'

'Is that all you can say?' Howard burst out.

'What do you expect me to say?' Alexis shook his head. 'Give me a chance to take it in.'

'You're to fly home first thing in the morning,' went on Howard grimly. 'I want you here, in my office, before noon.'

'I'll think about it,' Alexis was controlling his own anger now. 'I'm not a boy any more, Howard. Don't try to give me orders!'

'Alex!' There was a short explosive silence, and then his father went on more reasonably: 'Alex, for God's sake, man, do as I ask. I have to talk to you. And not like this.'

'Where's Janie?'

Howard snorted furiously. 'You're not still interested in her, are you?'

'No.' Alexis was cool. 'But as one human being to another, I guess I can feel sympathy for her, can't I? Or don't you know what that is?'

'I shouldn't waste my sympathies on her,' retorted Howard brutally. 'But as far as I know, she's still at the apartment.'

'Did she—?'

'—find her husband? No.' Howard was definite about that. 'He took an overdose of drugs at the office. The night watchman found him. He telephoned her.'

'I see.' Alexis digested this. 'Okay, okay, don't distress yourself. I'll fly back tomorrow. But I don't see what there is to get so steamed up about.'

'Don't you?' Howard caught his breath. 'Well, maybe you will tomorrow. You think about it, right?'

'Right.' Alexis reached for a cigar and put it between his teeth. 'Is that all?'

'Isn't it enough?'

Alexis lit the cigar and inhaled deeply. 'Fine. See you some time before dinner. That's the best I can promise,' and he rang off.

He smoked his cigar thoughtfully for a while, and then stubbing it out went back into the bathroom to finish drying his hair. When he returned to the bedroom he had put on a towelling bathrobe and he flung himself on the wide bed and stared up at the ceiling. His father's call had banished all thoughts of sleep he might have had, and he felt a rising sense of frustration at the inadequacy of the information he had been given. But then telephones were not particularly confidential pieces of equipment and he supposed he could understand his father's reluctance to be too explicit. Even so, it was an unsatisfactory state of affairs.

He thought about Janie Knight. He hadn't seen her since the beginning of December last year, which must be about six weeks ago now. Of course, after he had stopped seeing her, she had telephoned him, numerous times, and even visited his apartment, although Drake, his man-servant, knew better than to let her in. She had not been able to accept that it was all over, and he had hoped these weeks at Grüssmatte would convince her irrevocably that he meant what he said. And now this had happened, and while he didn't feel any sense of blame, it left a nasty taste in his mouth.

David Vanning was most put out the next morning when Alexis broke the news to him that he was leaving as they had breakfast together.

'But, Alex, we've only been here a couple of weeks. Surely your old man can do without you for longer than that!'

Alexis smiled rather ruefully. 'It seems not, Dave. I'm sorry, but there it is. Still, I guess Rosemary will find the time to console you!'

David made a helpless gesture. 'That's not the point, Alex. Rosemary's okay; you know I'm very keen on her, and I guess one day we'll get married and all that, but – well, she's no athlete, and I don't intend to spend the rest of my holiday hanging round the hotel or making shopping excursions into Innsbruck.'

Alexis rested his elbow on the table, supporting his chin on one hand. 'Do I detect a note of dissatisfaction in your voice?' he queried lazily. 'Surely the romantic idyll hasn't begun to pall already?'

David looked slightly embarrassed. 'It's not that. It's just that – well, her parents are always around. We never get any time alone. Not really alone, that is.'

Alexis looked amused. 'Well, that's what comes of doing things by the book.'

'What do you mean? Coming here with her parents?'

'More or less.'

'They'd never have let her come away with me alone.'

'Hard luck!'

'I suppose you think in my position you'd have managed to persuade them.'

'I didn't say that.'

'No, but you thought it.' David lifted his shoulders dejectedly. 'Hell, Alex, is it absolutely essential that you leave today?'

'Absolutely, I'm afraid.' Alexis finished his second cup

of coffee looking idly through the restaurant window on to the groups of holidaymakers making their way towards the ski slopes. 'I suppose I ought to go and see how they're getting on with my packing. I shall be sorry to leave all this.'

David grimaced. 'I half wish I was coming with you.'

Alexis's lips lifted at his friend's outburst, but then his attention was arrested by a sleek continental coach that was slowly progressing along the village street. He was suddenly reminded that the girl he had met last night in such unusual circumstances had said she and her group were leaving today. The coach was most probably for them.

'Did you hear what I said?'

David's irate tones brought his attention back to the present and he looked at him apologetically. 'No. What did you say?'

'I said I'd ring you once I got back to London.'

'Oh, yes, yes. Fine.' But Alexis was preoccupied. He rose abruptly to his feet. 'I've got to get moving. What are your plans for this morning?'

David lay back in his chair shrugging. 'I don't know. I've been promising to take Rosemary on the nursery slopes for days. I guess I could do that.'

Alexis nodded, and then with a sense of compunction he patted David's shoulder. 'I'm sorry, man. But there's nothing I can do.' He paused. 'Be seeing you, then.'

'Yes. Sure.'

David nodded, managing a faint smile, but as Alex crossed the restaurant to reach the hall, he could see David's dejected reflection in the long mirrors that flanked the swing glass doors.

The flight from Salzburg landed in the late afternoon. It had been delayed by bad weather conditions, and it was even snowing slightly at Heathrow as Alexis left the plane.

The formalities over with, he emerged from the reception lounge bent on finding the nearest bar and a stiff drink. He knew he was delaying the moment when he would have to take up his life again, but airports were those transient kind of places where one was in limbo, a condition he presently desired.

But as he climbed the stairs to the bar, a voice he recognized only too well, called: 'Alex! Alex, where are you going?'

He halted reluctantly and turned, looking down into the well of the hall where a fur-clad feminine figure was waving vigorously at him. He hesitated only a moment, and then with resignation descended the stairs again. He knew perfectly well that had he pretended not to hear her and gone on to the bar, she would have followed him.

Reaching ground level, he turned up the collar of his sheepskin coat against the cold draught of air which swept through the hall, and said, in drawling tones: 'Hello, Michelle. What are you doing here?'

Michelle Whitney smiled up at him warmly. She was an attractive woman of medium height, but wrapped in the expensive sables she looked particularly elegant. 'Alex darling,' she cried reprovingly. 'Where else would I be? I've come to meet you, of course. Your father sent me. I've been waiting around for simply hours!'

Alexis considered her avid expression without enthusiasm. 'That wasn't necessary, Michelle. I'm quite capable of hiring a cab.'

Michelle raised her delicately plucked eyebrows. 'What a greeting! It's just as well I'm used to your boorishness, darling, or I'd feel quite hurt.'

Alexis's lips were wry. 'Is that possible?' he queried mockingly, and was gratified to see her colour deepen.

'Oh, you are a pig, Alex!' she exclaimed heatedly. 'I don't know why I put up with it.'

'Don't you?' He glanced round irritably. 'Look, Michelle, I want a drink and as I'm perfectly certain that my father did not send you to meet me, in fact I don't know how you got the information—'

'I was there when your father phoned you last night!'

'Okay, I'll accept that. But now, I suggest you go home, and I'll see you both later.'

Michelle wrapped her fur-clad arms closely about herself. 'Why can't I have a drink with you?'

'Because I want to be alone.'

'Alex, please!'

'No.' He half turned away and then looked back at her. 'Don't worry. Your little secret's safe with me. I won't tell the old man.'

Michelle pursed her lips. 'There are times when I hate you, Alex!'

'Good. That's a healthy emotion.'

'All my emotions towards you are healthy, Alex.' She put a tentative hand on his arm.

Alex looked down at that soft-gloved hand, and then into her face, and with a muffled gasp she released him. 'I still don't see why we can't have a drink together. I am your stepmother, after all.'

'Yes. Unfortunately I'm aware of that,' retorted Alexis, brutally. 'G'-bye, Michelle. I'll see you later, at home.'

Without another word, he swung back up the stairs, and didn't look back, not even as he walked along the gallery.

Alexis's apartment was the penthouse of a tall block near Hyde Park, and Blake, his manservant, welcomed him home warmly some two hours later. As Alexis shed his coat in the hall of the apartment Blake said: 'Your father's been on the phone for you, sir. Several times. I told him you hadn't arrived back yet, but I'm not sure he believed me. He said he had telephoned the airport, and he knew your plane had landed some time ago.'

Alexis grimaced, and unfastening his tie, he walked ahead into the wide, attractive lounge. This was a room that always gave him pleasure and he looked about him with enjoyment, appreciating its comfortable elegance. There was a turquoise carpet underfoot, patterned in shades of blue and green, while the long settee and armchairs were natural-coloured, soft, buttoned leather. He was lucky enough to be able to afford all the luxurious accoutrements to modern living, but the massive television was seldom turned on, and in recent years his interest in the hi-fi equipment, which had once fascinated him, had dwindled.

Now Blake came behind him, carrying his suitcase. 'Have you had dinner, sir?' he asked.

Alexis turned from switching on a tall standard lamp, that had an exquisitely hand-painted shade, and frowned. 'No, I've not eaten. I had a couple of drinks at the airport, that's all.' He took off the jacket of his suit and slung it carelessly over the back of a chair. 'But don't bother with anything for me. I'll eat at Falcons.' Falcons was the name of his father's house at Maidenhead.

'Are you sure, sir? It's no trouble.'

Alexis smiled. 'No, I know. Thanks all the same. But I need a shower, and quite honestly hunger is not one of the things that's troubling me at the moment.'

Blake nodded politely. 'Did you have a good holiday, sir?'

Alexis considered before replying. 'Yes, I suppose you could say that,' he conceded grudgingly. 'By the way, make me some coffee, will you, and I'll have it after I'm dressed again. It won't do to arrive smelling too strongly of alcohol.'

Blake allowed himself a smile at that. He was rather a solemn-faced individual, and as he was inclined to stockiness and was going bald, he did not at first strike one as being particularly amiable. But in fact, he had been with Alexis for six years now, and Alexis was well aware of the sharp sense of humour he possessed. Now, he collected Alexis's casually strewn jacket before disappearing through a door into the kitchen, and Alexis walked across to his bedroom.

In the shower, Alexis contemplated the evening ahead without pleasure. How much more enjoyable it would have been to arrive home and have nothing more pressing to do than lounge on the couch in front of the television all evening. Such a prospect attracted him. It was strange that someone who should become so easily bored with the so-called fleshpots, should find the idea of simply behaving like any one of another hundred million people so desirable.

He examined his reflection in the bathroom mirror as he dried himself and was relieved to see that the past couple of weeks of exertion had successfully dispersed the faint thickening of his waistline that had been present before he left. Now there wasn't an ounce of spare flesh on his lean body, and the outline of his rib cage was coated only with muscle.

He dressed soberly in a charcoal grey lounge suit, to fit the occasion, he thought without humour, and drove down to Maidenhead, reaching his father's house just before eight o'clock. Falcons faced the river, and in summer it was very pleasant to sit in the garden, watching the pageant of craft on the water. But in the middle of January, it had no such connotations, and although Alexis had spent part of his childhood here, he found the sight of the bare trees and the frozen, snow-covered gardens rather depressing.

Searle, his father's manservant, admitted him. Once Searle had had the title of butler, but in these days of shortages of staff, his duties encompassed so many other things, that such an appellation would have sounded pretentious. However, the old man seemed not to mind, and he welcomed Alexis warmly.

'It's good to see you again, sir,' he exclaimed, taking his overcoat.

'How are you, Searle?' Alexis bestowed one of his rare

warm smiles upon him.

'Can't grumble, sir. Mr. Howard's waiting for you in the library.'

'Has my father had dinner?'

'Not yet, sir. He's been waiting for you.'

'Good.' Alexis found that the drive had awakened his appetite. 'Thank you, Searle.'

He crossed the hall to double panelled doors, and taking a handle in each hand, he swung them open and stepped into the book-lined room which his father used as his study.

Howard Whitney was seated behind his desk, and he looked up dourly as Alexis closed the doors behind him and leaned back against them, surveying the room thoroughly.

'So you've finally decided to appear!' he remarked grimly. 'Not before time!'

Howard Whitney's voice still had traces of his northern ancestry that no amount of southern intonation could entirely dispel. He rose from his desk to face his son, and in his dark evening clothes he was quite impressive, big and broad and physically dominating.

But Alexis was never dominated. He was as tall as his father and although he was leaner, it was a leanness of muscle and sinew that was far tougher than his father's loose flesh.

'I got held up,' he said now. 'Besides, I don't see why I should account to you for my movements. I'm not a boy.'

'No, you're not!' muttered Howard, reaching for a cigar, but refraining to offer one to Alexis. 'If you were, you wouldn't create the kind of mess we're in at the moment.'

'What do you mean?' Alexis moved away from the door.

'I mean Janie Knight, Alex.'

Alexis frowned. 'I seem to have missed something

along the way. As I recall it, last night we were discussing Frank Knight, not Janie.'

'It's all the same thing,' retorted Howard. 'My God, what is there about you that makes a woman like Janie Knight prepared to go to any lengths to get you back?'

Alexis glanced across at the tray of drinks on a side table. 'Perhaps you'd better start at the beginning,' he advised dryly. 'Do you mind if I have a drink?'

'Help yourself!' said Howard Whitney irritably, and Alexis poured himself a generous measure of Scotch. 'Go on!' he said.

Howard shuffled the papers on his desk. 'I wish to God you'd never got involved with her!'

Alexis swallowed half his drink, surveying the remainder in his glass thoughtfully. 'It was your idea,' he pointed out.

Howard clenched his fists. 'Do you think I'm likely to forget that?'

'Well?'

'Knight left a note – a suicide note.'

'I see.' Alexis was beginning to understand. 'Where is it? Have the press got it?'

'Nothing so simple. Janie's got it. When the night watchman phoned her about Knight's attempted suicide, she was first on the scene, before the ambulance or the police. She took the note, and she still has it.'

'You mean she's attempting blackmail?' Alexis frowned. 'What does it say, for God's sake?'

His father heaved a deep sigh. There were lines of strain around his mouth and it was obvious he was most disturbed. 'Well, he mentions the difficulties his company has got into, and how he can see no future short of selling out to a larger corporation. He apparently owes money all over the city.'

'But that's not what's worrying you, is it?' Alexis was impatient.

'No. No, he goes on to say that – he knows his wife is

being unfaithful to him, and that she's – the mistress of the son of the man who has been systematically trying to ruin him!'

Alexis finished his Scotch and replaced the glass on the tray, wiping his mouth with the back of his hand. For a few minutes he said nothing, and then, when his father was beginning to get agitated, he asked: 'Have you seen this letter?'

Howard Whitney frowned. 'What kind of a fool do you think I am? Of course I've seen the letter.'

'When?'

'Yesterday evening. In my office.'

'You mean Janie Knight walked into your office with the actual letter her husband wrote?' Alexis gave his father an old-fashioned look. 'Wasn't she afraid you'd take it from her?'

Howard sighed. 'She wasn't alone.'

'You mean someone else knows about this?'

'Yes. That chap Lorrimer – her lawyer.'

'Philip Lorrimer?' Alexis shook his head. 'I wouldn't trust him as far as I could throw him!'

'Maybe not, but there it is.'

'But how can you be sure the letter was written by Knight?'

'If it wasn't, it's a damn good facsimile. Good enough to fool me!'

'But not good enough to fool a handwriting expert.'

'My God, Alex, what good is that? Even if the whole thing is a hoax, even if we take them to court and prove it's a hoax, it's going to cause a God-awful stink, and that's something I could do without right now.'

'Oh, yes.' Alexis was bitter. 'It wouldn't do to jeopardize your knighthood for services to industry, would it? That's quite a pun, isn't it?'

'Shut up, Alex! If it wasn't for you there'd be no mess.'

'What do you mean?' Alexis was indignant. 'I wasn't

responsible for buying up the shares in Knight's company – you were.'

'I know it, I know it. But don't you see, if Janie Knight wasn't so infatuated with you, she'd never have contacted me the way she did. She'd have been just as eager to hush up a scandal as I am.'

'So what's the deal?' Alexis was wary.

'It's quite simple really. She wants you back again.'

'You can't be serious!' Alexis was half amused.

'Can't I?' But Howard was not joking. 'She said you love her – you love one another! You only gave her up because Knight's company was practically ruined, and I told you to do so.'

'Nobody tells me what to do,' muttered Alexis grimly.

His father made a frustrated gesture. 'I did tell her that, but to no avail, I'm afraid. You must have done your job well. I only asked for information – not recruits!'

But Alexis was not amused. 'Well, whatever her terms, they're unacceptable.'

'I was afraid you'd say that. Alex—'

'*No*, Howard! Not now – not ever!'

Howard sank down wearily into his chair. 'She'll give it to the press.'

'*If* there is a letter. Personally, I have my doubts. It's too convenient. Anyway, let her do it. I know who'll come off worst in the long run. Besides, what she did, she did for herself, not for me.'

Howard shook his head. 'And what do you intend to do?'

'Me? About this? Nothing.'

Howard riffled through his papers. 'I think it would be a good idea if you returned to Austria. With you out of the way, I might be able to salvage something from the mess.'

'I do not intend to return to Austria!' stated Alexis coldly. 'Quite honestly, I'm sick of the whole bloody round of social back-stabbing. Particularly when there are women involved!'

His father looked up in surprise. 'What's got into you?'

Alexis shook his head, and at that moment Michelle Whitney chose to appear. In a long gown of pale green slipper satin that showed off her rounded figure to advantage she was very attractive, and her eyes slid greedily over Alexis's deeply tanned skin before moving on to her husband.

'Aren't you nearly finished, darling?' she asked, perching on a corner of Howard's desk and running her fingers down his cheek, looking deliberately in Alexis's direction as she did so. 'I'm dying of hunger.'

Howard rose, flexing his back muscles tiredly. 'Yes, we're finished, my dear.'

Michelle's eyes flickered towards her stepson. 'Hello, Alex. It's good to see you back again. Did you enjoy your holiday?'

Alexis inclined his head. 'Very much, thank you.'

'You can tell Searle to start serving now,' went on Howard, and Michelle slid off the desk. But although she looked once more at Alexis he seemed to find the pattern of the carpet more than absorbing and she was forced to look away.

After she had gone, Howard turned to his son, and frowned. 'Look here,' he said. 'Did you mean what you said just now? About being sick of playing around?'

Alexis was cautious. 'Why?'

'Well, old Jeff Pierce retired last week and so far they've not got anyone to take his job.'

'Jeff Pierce?' Alexis stared at his father. 'You mean – the manager at Wakeley?'

'That's right.' Howard was watching his son's reactions closely. 'How does it strike you? Being section manager in a woollen mill?'

Alexis ran a hand round the back of his neck. His

26

father's suggestion had left him temporarily stunned. It was something he had never even contemplated. He had worked in the company offices in London, of course, he had even taken a degree in economics at university, but to actually enter into the practical side of the business was something entirely different.

'But I know nothing about wool!'

'You don't have to. Business acumen is what's needed.'

'I suppose it would get me out of the way just as effectively,' he remarked dryly.

His father looked embarrassed. 'You did say you were sick of the same old round,' he defended himself.

'Yes, I did say that.' Alexis was thoughtful. 'But this! This is something else.'

'Don't you think you'll be able to do it? I'm not putting you in sole charge of the mill, you know. You'll have to answer to Jim Summerton if anything goes wrong, just as John McMullen does.'

Alexis gave a wry smile. 'Thank you for your confidence.'

'No, seriously though, Alex, what do you think?'

Alexis allowed his hand to fall to his side. 'I don't know. I really don't. I'd have to give the matter some thought.'

'I realize that. But it does – appeal to you, doesn't it?' Howard looked at him searchingly and Alexis raised his eyebrows.

'It's a challenge,' he conceded at last. 'It's a long time since I visited Wakeley. Must be six – maybe seven years. While I was at university, I guess. I remember going to see old John McMullen . . .'

Howard nodded vigorously. 'That's right.' He paused. 'To think – we used to live in Wakeley. Must be all of twenty years ago.' He shook his head. 'That house your mother liked so much – I wonder if it's still standing.'

Alexis's jaw hardened. 'Yes. Well, that's another story,

isn't it, Howard?'

His father breathed hard down his nose. 'You won't ever let me forget, will you, Alex?' he muttered, and looked up to find Michelle standing by the door.

'Forget what, darling?' she queried silkily, looking from one to the other of them curiously. 'Aren't you coming?'

Howard walked round the desk to join his wife, glancing at his son with scarcely concealed appeal. 'Yes, we're coming, Michelle.' He tucked her hand through his arm. 'And what delicacy have you had prepared for us this evening?'

Alexis followed them through to the dining-room, but he was preoccupied with what he and his father had been discussing, and he sensed Michelle's impatience that she had been excluded from their discussions.

CHAPTER TWO

KAREN could hear her father's voice raised in anger as she entered the house, and a frown came to mar her wide brow. It was unusual to hear Daniel Sinclair so heated about anything, and dropping the pile of exercise books she had brought home to mark on to the hall table, she pushed open the door and entered the living-room.

Her parents were standing on the hearth before the roaring fire. The room had a cosy lived-in warmth which was presently belied by the coldness of her father's expression. Karen looked at them both questioningly, noting her mother's worried frown, and then said:

'So what's happened? I could hear you shouting halfway down the street, Pop!'

'Don't call me Pop!' muttered her father irritably. 'And I wasn't shouting. I was merely exhibiting my frustration, that's all.'

Karen dropped down into an armchair near the fire, holding out her cold hands to the flames. 'What have you got to feel frustrated about?' she asked, a trace of humour about her mouth.

Daniel Sinclair reached for his pipe off the mantelshelf and put it between his teeth with obvious intolerance. 'I have my reasons!'

Karen made a move, and looked at her mother. 'What's happened? Have I done something?'

'No, of course not.' Laura Sinclair shook her head, and gave her husband an impatient look. Then she turned her attention to her daughter. 'You look frozen! Didn't you get a lift home?'

Karen shook her head. 'No. Ray had to go into Wakefield, so I said there was no point in him coming out of his way in weather like this. It's snowing again, you know. I caught the bus, but it was late as usual.'

Her mother listened, nodding, but Karen could tell her thoughts were still occupied with her husband's affairs. 'I thought you were later than usual,' she said, glancing at the clock. 'The meal won't take long. It's a chicken casserole. Are you hungry?'

'Ravenous!' Karen smiled, and then made a puzzled gesture towards her father. 'What's going on? Why was Daddy so upset when I came in?' She paused. 'The – the mill's not closing down or anything, is it?'

Daniel Sinclair turned on her. 'Now why should you think a thing like that?' he demanded aggressively.

Karen was taken aback. 'No reason, Pop. It's not, is it?'

'No, of course not.' Her father chewed irritably at the end of his pipe.

Karen sighed with relief. With so many firms closing down it had been a very real possibility. 'So what is it?'

'Jeff Pierce's job has been filled!' snapped her father.

Karen digested this before saying any more. 'And – and you've not been considered?'

'Damn right!' Daniel snorted angrily. 'It's a disgrace!'

Karen hesitated. 'Ian Halliday hasn't got it, has he?' Halliday was her father's assistant.

'No. I could almost wish he had.'

Karen sighed. 'Then who has got it?' She couldn't think of anyone else with the qualifications.

'Only that playboy son of Howard Whitney's, who's always getting his name into the papers for one fool thing after another!'

Karen felt some of the colour draining out of her cheeks, and hastily covered them with her palms, her elbows resting on her knees. She didn't want her parents to notice her sudden sense of shock. 'Not – not Alexis Whitney?' she murmured, controlling the tremor in her voice.

30

But fortunately no one noticed her. 'Yes, that's the chap,' said her father bitterly. 'What in God's name he wants to come to a place like this for I'll never know! The life he's been leading these past few years, I shouldn't have thought Wakeley would be big enough to hold him!'

Laura Sinclair put a calming hand on her husband's arm. 'Stop getting yourself so angry about it, Dan!' she exclaimed. 'There's nothing you can do about it, so you might as well try and make the best of it. If, as you say, he's not the type to take to discipline, then no doubt he won't stick it long.'

Daniel thrust his pipe into the pocket of his cardigan. 'What I can't understand is why he should be coming here in the first place. Oh, I know there's been all that gossip in the press about him and some company director's wife recently, but Howard Whitney should know better than to send him here.'

'But they used to live here,' said Laura mildly.

'Yes, years ago. Before Howard made his pile. D'you think they'd live here now? No, by God! We'd not be good enough for them.' He shook his head. 'But sending that spoiled brat here to be manager, to take over from old Jeff, to even take over his house! Well, it's downright disgraceful!'

'He's hardly a brat any longer, Dan,' remarked Laura dryly. 'He must be almost thirty.'

'That's not the point.' Her husband brought out his pipe again and put it between his teeth. 'What does he know about the job? What does he know about wool! Bloody layabout!'

While her parents went on and on arguing about the new appointment, Karen sat as though frozen in her chair. And she was frozen, mentally at least. Two or three weeks ago, before the school trip to Grüssmatte, this news would have caused her a momentary pang, and then been forgotten. What was past was past, and she would

31

have got on with her life without too much soul-search-
ing.

But ten days ago she had come face to face with a ghost
from the past, a ghost she realized had haunted her for
years, and she had known that far from being forgotten,
he had merely been hidden behind the veils of memory
she had deliberately allowed to fall.

Alexis Whitney! She shivered. How much more angry
her father would be about this appointment if he knew
how closely Alexis Whitney had come to ruining his own
daughter's life. Her lips twisted. Had she changed so
much as to be unrecognizable? Or had there been so
many in his life that her face paled to insignificance
beside others more beautiful?

Her parents' conversation was breaking up. Her father
was leaning down to switch on the television, and her
mother was going out to dish up their evening meal in the
kitchen. Karen got rather jerkily to her feet, and turning
her attention to her father she said, in what she hoped
were casual tones: 'And when does the prodigal
arrive?'

Daniel had taken his seat before the television and was
concentrating on the programme so that she had to
repeat herself before he answered shortly: 'What? Oh,
tomorrow, so I hear. He was in with Jim Summerton this
afternoon.'

Karen stifled a gasp. 'You mean he's here in Wakeley
already?'

Her father looked up, clearly not happy about being
distracted. 'That's what I said. What's the matter with
you, girl? It won't affect you, will it? Whether he's here
or not.'

Karen flushed then. 'Of course not. I was merely showing interest, that's all.'

'Well, you keep your interests occupied elsewhere. I
wouldn't have any daughter of mine involved with a rake
like him.' Daniel surveyed her critically. 'Hmm, I've no

doubt he'd find you to his taste! Short skirts, long skirts, all that loose hair! Don't the education authorities care that their staff should look more mature than the pupils? My God, in my day, teachers were teachers, not bits of girls in clothes designed to attract trouble!'

Karen managed to smile at this. 'Oh, Pop, don't be so silly. Nobody cares about things like that nowadays. It's what the pupils absorb that matters, not what they see.'

'And they see plenty, if you ask me!' muttered her father grimly. 'How old are those boys you teach? Fifteen, sixteen? I don't know how you get them to take any notice of you.'

'I manage,' remarked Karen, and escaped to the kitchen to help her mother dish up the dinner.

'Is Ray coming round tonight?' Laura asked, as she added butter to the potatoes.'

Karen shrugged, her appetite depleted by her father's attitude. 'I expect so,' she agreed, lifting the lid of the casserole and allowing a rich odour of chicken and herbs to pervade the atmosphere. 'He had to go and see about the new instruments. Apparently there's been some hold-up or something.'

'He's a very conscientious young man,' observed her mother approvingly. 'Everyone said at Christmas how much the choir's improved since he took it over.'

'Yes.' Karen spoke absently, moving about the room lifting a piece of cutlery here, a dish there, generally annoying her mother until Laura said sharply:

'What's the matter with you? You're not worrying about your father, are you?'

Karen looked up guiltily. Her father had been far from her thoughts just then. 'Why – no! Of course not.'

'That's good, because I don't think I could cope with two of you! For heaven's sake, somebody had to get Jeff Pierce's job. It could quite easily have been young Ian Halliday. After all, your father's only got a few years to go to retirement, whereas Ian's only in his thirties.'

Karen shrugged. 'But Pop said he would rather it had been Ian!'

'Don't you believe it. If Ian Halliday had got the job, there'd have been some hard words said, believe you me.'

'So he'd have been just as angry whoever got it?'

'Oh, no, I wouldn't go so far as to say that. Your father's never really cared for Howard Whitney being so successful. They were boys together here in Wakeley, and while Howard's father owned a mill even in those days, he never made a lot of money. It took Howard's brain and know-how to make Whitney Textiles what it is today.'

'I see.' Karen digested this slowly. 'Does Pop know Howard Whitney, then?'

'Of course he does. He visits Wakeley occasionally—'

'No, I didn't mean that. I meant – did he know him well?'

Laura shrugged, lifting hot plates from under the grill. 'Well, when they were younger they knew one another. And even after Howard got married, they used to occasionally have a drink together, that sort of thing. But then the business developed, Howard was away a lot, and eventually they moved to London. Of course, Howard's first wife is dead now, and he's married again. Some ex-fashion model, or something. I remember reading about it seven or eight years ago. Your father was disgusted about that, too, I remember. Howard's wife had been dead scarcely a year at the time.'

Karen listened with interest, wishing her mother would go on. But Laura was going through to the dining-room now, putting plates and dishes on the table, and Karen had, perforce, to help her. Then, her father was called through to join them, and to her mother's obvious relief the conversation turned to more general topics.

It was Wednesday, and Karen's parents usually went to play bridge at the home of some friends on Wednesday evenings, so after they had gone Karen decided to wash

34

her hair. It was snowing quite heavily now, and she didn't think Ray would come round after all.

However, just as she was finishing rinsing her hair, the doorbell rang. Hastily wrapping a towel turban-wise round her head, she pulled on her navy quilted dressing-gown and ran downstairs. She pulled open the door to a flurry of snow, and then smiled as Ray Nichols stepped swiftly inside.

Closing the door, she exclaimed: 'I thought you weren't coming. Do you realize it's after nine o'clock!'

Ray raised his dark eyebrows at her towel-swathed hair. 'What a greeting!' he commented, 'although . . .' He surveyed her more thoroughly, noticing the dark blue gown with approval. 'Very nice. Very nice indeed.'

Karen pointed to the living-room. 'Wait in there while I put some clothes on,' she said, and Ray bent to kiss her lips before complying.

His kiss was warm and gentle, and Karen responded without effort. He was an attractive young man, a little above medium build with square muscular shoulders and dark curly hair.

'Why bother?' he asked, when he lifted his head. 'I like you the way you are.'

Karen tugged the securing towel off her head, and her hair fell in wet coiling strands to her shoulders, black, and as silky soft as a raven's wing. 'And what do you think my father would say if he came back and found me like this?' she demanded.

Ray shrugged. 'Who cares? Sooner or later, he'll have to accept it, won't he?'

'What do you mean?'

'I mean – when we're married,' replied Ray quietly.

Karen stared at him in amazement. 'Are you pro-posing, Ray? Here? In the hall?'

'What would you have me do? Get down on my knees?' Ray shook her gently. 'Karen, you know how I feel about you. It's been obvious for months. And I think you feel

35

the same.'

Karen's lips parted. It was strange that this evening, which had held so many surprises already, should still hold one more.

'I don't know, Ray,' she was beginning, when he put his hand over her mouth.

'Please, Karen, don't say anything yet. Think about it.'

Karen sighed. 'All right.' She glanced round awkwardly. 'Will you – er – go into the living-room? I won't be a minute.'

Ray hesitated, and then taking off his overcoat he slung it over the banister before opening the living-room door. Karen made her way thoughtfully upstairs. She ought not to have been surprised. She had been aware of Ray's feelings for her for some time. All her friends had commented upon it. But for all that, now that he had proposed, now that it had actually happened, she didn't know how to answer him.

She put up a hand to her wet hair. If she was really honest with herself, she would admit that the reason she was so unprepared for this today had little to do with Ray himself. It had to do with what had happened seven years ago, and with what her father had told them when she came home this afternoon.

She dressed in close-fitting velvet slacks and a purple sweater, rubbed her hair almost dry and left it hanging loosely about her cheeks, and then went downstairs again. In the living-room, Ray was relaxing in her father's armchair before the blazing fire, idly watching an American film thriller on the television.

She closed the door and he looked across at her with caressing eyes. Patting his knee, he said: 'Come here!'

Karen hesitated, and then walked slowly across to him, allowing him to pull her down on to his lap. She rested against him, and he nursed her like a child, his eyes drifting past her again to the television. Karen felt a sense of restlessness assail her. Although she and Ray had been going out together for almost two years, he had never once attempted to make love to her, other than the sometimes passionate little kisses they exchanged on greeting and parting. Not that she wanted him to seduce her, quite the contrary, but after listening to the sexual exploits of her friends she had the feeling that Ray was perhaps a little too cool. Maybe he was one of those men who didn't need that kind of stimulation, she pondered curiously, and then half smiled. That was the trouble with this generation, she thought. They were so brainwashed by films and television that they were constantly trying to psychoanalyse themselves, instead of accepting what they had and being grateful and letting nature take its course. It was debatable whether the modern idea of discussing everything was right. To those who did not share in that free-thinking revolution, there could be restlessness and dissatisfaction, just as Karen was feeling now.

Abruptly, she sat up, and Ray looked up at her in surprise. 'What's wrong?'

Karen hunched her shoulders. 'Nothing, I guess.'

Ray frowned. 'Yes, there is. What is it? Is it what I asked earlier?'

'Well – yes and no!'

'What do you mean?'

Karen paused. 'Ray, don't you ever get restless? I mean, aren't you ever tempted to – well, make love to me?'

Ray stared at her in amazement. Then he coloured. 'No,' he muttered roughly. 'I want to marry you.'

'I know that.' Karen sought about for words. 'It's just that – well, I sometimes think you're a pretty cold fish. I mean, you never go in for petting or that sort of thing, do you?'

Ray struggled up out of his lounging position. 'Come on, Karen,' he said. 'That's no way to talk. Imagine what your father would think if he could hear you now.'

37

Karen sighed 'I'm only talking. I'm not doing anything wrong. I don't even want to do anything wrong. I just wondered, that's all.'

Ray snorted. 'Well, it's just as well I'm not the sort of chap to take you up on it, that's all!' he said sharply.

Karen slid off his knees. 'I'll make some coffee,' she said, walking towards the door, and he made no move to stop her. Indeed, when she glanced back she saw that he was once more engrossed in the television.

Karen taught English and history at Wakeley Comprehensive School. She had been there for the past three years, ever since leaving university in fact, and she enjoyed her work tremendously. She was a popular girl with both staff and pupils, and as Ray taught at the same school they had a lot in common.

The following afternoon, Karen had some shopping to do before going home, and Ray dropped her in the High Street. Although he lived some distance from Karen's home, he invariably drove her back in the afternoons, and she was grateful. The buses, particularly at this time of the year, were notoriously unreliable.

Karen collected her mother's books from the library, bought herself some tights and cosmetics, and then walked briskly along towards the bus stop. The snow of the previous day had melted in the town centre and the pavements and roads were slushy and wet. Avoiding the edge of the path because of the filthy mess thrown up by the traffic, Karen's attention was caught by a sleek green sports limousine that was nosing its way along the High Street behind a heavy goods vehicle. The driver was unmistakably familiar, and she shrank back into a shop doorway, which was quite ridiculous really as in the deplorable weather conditions and the crowded pavements there was no possible chance of him noticing her.

Nevertheless, the small incident shook her, bringing it home to her forcibly that it would be comparatively easy to encounter him in a small place like Wakeley. Still, she consoled herself, he was hardly likely to go far without his car, and Leeds was much more his environment than anywhere else around here.

During the next few days, Karen had to get used to hearing her father talk about Alexis Whitney. Daniel was always grumbling about things the new manager was doing, but underlying that anger she sensed an anxious thread of concern, as though her father was afraid his methods were about to be supplanted. It became obvious that whatever his reasons for coming to Wakeley, Alexis was not prepared to sit back and allow his work to be done for him as Jeff Pierce had been inclined to do, and in consequence the whole section had felt his presence.

Karen knew her mother was concerned about the effect it was having on her husband, but there was nothing either of them could do. Daniel had refused to accept the situation with any degree of resignation, and began working longer hours, keeping his department constantly on its toes.

The weather continued very cold and Karen hated getting out of bed in the mornings. Not that she was prone to colds or sickness; on the contrary she seemed to thrive on the conditions, but her father did not. The way he was driving himself had weakened his resistance and one morning when Karen came down to breakfast she found her mother arguing hotly with him.

'You're mad!' she was saying, as Karen entered the dining-room. 'Mad! You'll give yourself pneumonia!'

'I'll be all right. Stop fussing, woman!' said Daniel hoarsely, and Karen looked at him with concern. His eyes were red-rimmed and watery, there were splashes of hectic colour in his cheeks, and his nose was sore from constant use of his handkerchief. He was obviously full of cold and when he started to cough she looked at her mother exasperatedly.

'Surely he doesn't intend to go to work!'

Laura shrugged, looking anxious. 'Try and stop him!'

'Stop talking about me as if I wasn't here,' exclaimed Daniel. 'I've got a cold, that's all. Everyone has colds at this time of the year. It's all this bad weather.'

Karen folded her arms. 'You look as though you've got 'flu to me!' she stated. 'Go back to bed, Pop. You look terrible!'

Her father got to his feet, pushing aside his unfinished plate of bacon and eggs. 'Lord spare me from women!' he muttered, raising his eyes heavenward. 'There's nothing wrong with me that a couple of aspirin won't cure. You can get them for me, Laura, while I put on my coat.'

Laura made a resigned gesture and turned away to do his bidding, while Karen shrugged and then dropped down into a chair at the table. She was buttering some toast, which was all she wanted, when her father came back, wearing his coat, a muffler round his neck. She looked up at him worriedly.

'You will take care, won't you, Pop?'

Daniel's expression softened. 'Of course I will. I've told you, it's just a cold.'

But when Karen arrived home from school that afternoon she found the doctor just leaving the house. Giving him a polite smile, she followed her mother indoors and then exclaimed: 'Is it Pop? What's happened?'

Her mother gave her a resigned look. 'Nothing drastic. Your father was taken ill at work this afternoon, and that Mr. Whitney insisted he came home. Ian Halliday brought him in his car.'

'Oh!' Karen's lips parted. 'What did the doctor say, then?'

'It's 'flu, just like you said. He was a fool to go anywhere today. Anyway, he's really done it now. The doctor insists that he stays in bed for at least three days.' She stifled a chuckle. 'You should have seen his face when Dr. Thomas said that.'

Karen took off her coat. 'Well, I'm relieved it's nothing more serious.'

'So am I. If he hadn't come home it could have developed into pleurisy or pneumonia. It's no use. He's not a young man any more, and he can't play around with his health.'

'I'll go up and see him.'

Karen left her mother and ran lightly up the stairs. Entering her parents' bedroom she found her father lying with his eyes closed looking somehow vulnerable. A surge of compassion welled up inside her, but then his eyes opened and it fled as he said harshly:

'What a mess this is!'

'You're only where you belong,' Karen declared lightly. 'Good heavens, you weren't fit to go to work.'

'Maybe not, but I don't need a manager to tell me what to do!'

'I'm sure – Mr. Whitney only did what he thought was best,' she remarked cautiously.

'Best for him, you mean.' Her father moved restlessly in the bed. 'Sending me home like that. Calling the doctor.'

'Did he do that?' Karen was surprised.

' 'Course he did. You don't think I'd have let your mother call him, do you?'

'Perhaps he knew that,' murmured Karen quietly.

'Huh!' Her father sounded bitter. 'Anyway, I'm out of the way now for goodness knows how long! He'll be able to do as he likes and no one to stand in his way.'

'Oh, Pop! I'm sure you're exaggerating.'

'What do you know about it? And I've told you before, don't call me Pop!'

Karen sighed. 'Do you want a cup of tea?'

'No. I don't want anything.' Her father began to cough hoarsely, and she watched him helplessly until he lay spent upon the pillows. 'All right, all right,' he muttered. 'I'll have some tea.'

Karen hesitated only a moment longer and then left him. In this mood there was no reasoning with him.

After the evening meal, her mother said: 'I promised I'd go down to Lucy's this evening. She's got a pattern for a dress and she asked if I'd help her cut it out. Do you think your father would mind?'

'Of course not.' Karen shook her head. 'Besides, I shall be here. I'm not going out. I expect Ray will come round later.'

Her mother looked at her uncertainly. 'Well, he's asleep at the moment. If I go now, I might be back before he wakes up.'

Karen gave her an exasperated smile. 'Darling, no one's going to need you for a couple of hours. Go on, go and chat to Lucy; tell her all about Daddy.'

Laura smiled, taking off her apron. 'It would be nice,' she admitted.

'There you are, then.' Karen lounged into a chair near the fire. 'Actually, I have some books to mark and I want to work out tomorrow's schedules.'

Laura nodded. 'All right. But I'll be as quick as I can.'

'Fine.' Karen glanced up as her mother left the room and then settled down to reading a fifteen-year-old's idea of the reasons behind the collapse of every empire since the days of Kubla Khan. Once she got up and switched on the record player, seducing herself with the rhythmic sound of a jazz piano.

When the doorbell rang she felt a sense of impatience. It was nearly nine o'clock and she had felt convinced that Ray would not come this evening. He knew she had work to do.

Glancing down at her crumpled velvet pants and loose white smock, she sighed. Oh well, she thought resignedly, she hadn't time to change now. Running a smoothing hand over her straight hair, she went to the door and swung it open.

But it was not Ray Nichols who stood on the doorstep. It was a man, certainly, but he was taller and leaner, and the shafted light from the hall glinted on silvery lights in hair that was unmistakable.

Karen's heart thumped heavily. Sooner or later, she had known that this would happen, and now it had she felt totally inadequate. He was so much more attractive now than he had been seven years ago, lines of experience adding maturity to his features. And his holiday in Austria had given him a tan which was quite startling when his hair was so pale. But he didn't have the usual skin that went with such blondness, and he suffered none of the difficulties experienced by people with fair skin. Oh God, she thought weakly, to think she had once gone out with him, and once planned to go away with him for the weekend, alone . . .

CHAPTER THREE

'GOOD evening,' he was saying now, in that lazily attractive voice she remembered so well. 'I just called to see – *my God*!' He stared at her in astonishment, and she felt the hot colour run up her cheeks.

'Good – good evening, Mr. Whitney.'

His eyes narrowed, strange, amber eyes, like the eyes of a cat, with thick black lashes. 'I was right!' he said, almost to himself. 'We had met before, hadn't we?'

Karen thought quickly. 'I – er – of course. We met about a month ago in Grüssmatte.'

'I don't mean that,' he said, frowning. Then he shook his head. 'No matter.' He lifted his shoulders. 'The name – I should have guessed.'

Karen shivered. 'It's very cold, Mr. Whitney. What can I do for you?'

'You could invite me in,' he remarked dryly.

Karen was about to refuse, but then good manners stopped her. He was her father's superior, after all; the son of the mill owner, even if Howard Whitney had gone on to bigger and better things.

'Very well,' she stepped back. 'Won't you come in? My father's in bed, of course.'

'Naturally.'

Alexis stepped into the small hall which was immediately dwarfed by his presence. Karen felt disturbingly aware of him, and walked quickly ahead of him into the living-room. Gathering together her books which had been strewn all over the couch, she said: 'Please, sit down. Would you like a drink? There's only whisky, I'm afraid.'

Alexis unbuttoned his coat, but he didn't sit down. He stood on the hearth looking about the room, looking at her, until she felt hopelessly out of her depth.

'Whisky would be fine,' he agreed quietly. 'Tell me: how is your father?'

'Possibly better in health than temper,' she replied, pouring whisky into a glass from the sideboard cabinet. 'Do you have anything in this? Water – or ice?'

Alexis shook his head and she put the glass into his hand. 'That's fine, thank you.' He swallowed a mouthful, and then went on: 'Why do you say your father's angry? Because I sent him home?'

Karen twisted her hands together wishing he would sit down. 'I – I suppose so,' she replied, wishing she had not mentioned it. Her father wouldn't be very pleased if he knew what she had said.

Alexis nodded, looking down thoughtfully into his glass. Watching him, Karen was aware of every small detail about him, her eyes lingering on the fine material of the dark suit he was wearing, a dark grey fur-lined overcoat on top. His hands holding the glass were lean and hard and tanned, like the rest of him, and a disturbing feeling of apprehension ran through her. She had only been a young girl when she met him seven years ago – seventeen, little more than a child really. But she was a woman now, and whatever it was he had possessed then, he still possessed to a greater degree, and she did not intend to be foolish enough to tamper with it. Her own experience had taught her that if nothing else.

He looked up. 'I'm afraid your father doesn't like me.'

Karen glanced round apprehensively, half expecting her father to appear at any moment. But judging from the silence upstairs she could only assume he was still sleeping. 'I – er – I'm sure you're wrong.'

'No, I'm not. He doesn't think I know anything about the wool trade. He thinks this is only a game to me.'

'And isn't it?' The words were out before she could prevent them.

'No.' His brows were drawn together and suddenly he looked very formidable. 'I intend to do this job to the best of my ability, and it would make things a whole lot simpler if your father accepted this.'

Karen bent to pick up an errant exercise book. 'Well, it's nothing to do with me, Mr. Whitney.'

'Isn't it?' His tone was curt. 'I'm beginning to think it is.'

'What do you mean?' Her eyes were very wide and very blue.

'Surely it's obvious.' He finished the whisky in his glass and dropped it carelessly on to the mantelshelf. 'I'm the man who once tried to persuade his daughter to sleep with me!'

Karen's cheeks burned, and she pressed the palms of her hands to them. 'Don't say that!' she cried.

'Why not?' His lips curved derisively. 'You do remember, Karen, however much you try to deny it.'

'All right, all right.' Karen glanced fearfully over her shoulder, but there was no sound. 'All right, I remember. But – but my parents never learned the identity of – of the man!'

'Didn't they?' Alexis was ironic. 'I find that hard to believe.'

'Nevertheless, it's the truth.' Karen's hands dropped to her sides. 'Now, if you've said everything you came to say, perhaps you'd go!'

Alexis studied her intently, his eyes dropping down over her tall, slender young body with insolent appraisal. It was a devastating analysis, and Karen tensed. 'So you teach at the comprehensive school,' he remarked, at last.

'How do you know that?'

'Well, I could say that as you were escorting a party of teenagers in Grüssmatte, it was a reasonable assumption that you were a teacher, but I'll be honest and admit that John told me.'

'John?'

'McMullen.'

'Oh! The manager of the combing.'

'That's right.' Alexis removed his attention from her to pick up one of the exercise books she had left lying on the side table. 'The decline and fall of empire denotes a general decadence in administration,' he read, with amusement. 'Since when has decadence had a y?'

Karen held out her hand for the book, but he ignored it, and read on until Karen's nerves were stretched to screaming pitch. She stared at the clock on the mantelshelf behind him. It was nearly half past nine. Her mother had gone out soon after seven-thirty, surely she could not be much longer!

At last he dropped the book back on to the pile and gave her his attention again. 'Your father's in bed, I gather,' and at her nod, he went on: 'Did the doctor give any idea as to how long he would be away from work?'

Karen shrugged. 'He has to stay in bed at least three days. After that – I don't know. Perhaps one week, maybe two.'

'I see.' Alexis considered this thoughtfully. Then: 'And you? How are you? Recovered from your mountain expedition?'

Karen moved towards the door. 'I'm perfectly all right, thank you, Mr. Whitney. Are you?'

'Oh, yes. Fine.' He paused. 'Tell me something, did you recognize me in Grüssmatte?'

Karen sighed. 'I don't see that it matters.'

'It does to me.'

'Well, then – yes. Yes, I recognized you.'

'Why didn't you say so? You must have known when I questioned you I wasn't just making conversation.'

'How could I know that?'

'Damn you, because I don't need to employ that kind of an introduction,' he snapped, his temper aroused by her assumed indifference. Then, schooling himself, he

47

went on: 'I didn't immediately recognize you because you've changed.'

Karen put her hand on the door handle. 'I expect we all do that,' she managed in a casual tone.

Alexis studied her for a few agonizing moments longer, and then with a slight movement of his shoulders he walked to the door, stopping directly in front of her. 'Will you have dinner with me one evening?' he asked quietly, his eyes intent. 'Let's just say – for old times' sake.'

Karen took a backward step. 'I don't think that's a very good idea,' she replied, more calmly than she felt.

'Why not?'

Karen gestured towards the hall. 'Thank you for calling. I'll give my father your regards.'

'Karen!'

His tawny eyes darkened with anger, and she felt a tremor of awareness run through her, but even as she contemplated flight, the necessity for such a thing disappeared. A key turned in the lock, and a moment later Laura Sinclair stepped into the hall, brushing smudges of snow from her coat.

'Oh!' She stopped short at the sight of Karen and the tall stranger standing in the living-room doorway, and then exclaimed: 'Why, it's Mr. Whitney, isn't it?'

Alexis passed Karen then and went to shake hands with her mother, leaving her feeling suddenly bereft. 'That's right, Mrs. Sinclair,' he said politely. 'I just called to see how your husband was feeling.'

'That was kind of you.' Laura glanced towards her daughter. 'Have you been here long? Won't you stay and have some supper?'

'Mr. Whitney was just leaving,' said Karen quickly. 'Weren't you, Mr. Whitney?'

Alexis looked round at her. 'What?' His eyes narrowed, and for a heart-shaking moment she thought he was going to contradict her. 'Oh – yes, yes, I suppose I was. I'm sorry, Mrs. Sinclair. I – er – I have an appointment –

48

later.'

Laura gave an understanding smile. 'Of course. Anyway, it was thoughtful of you to take the trouble to come here at all. I'm sure Dan will appreciate it.'

'Are you?' Alexis sounded less assured about that. 'Well—' He looked again at Karen, but she bent her head, avoiding his eyes. 'It's been very nice meeting you both. Good night.'

'Good night.'

Laura opened the door for him and watched him walk down the path before closing it again. Then she turned to Karen, and her expression was less benign. 'What did he say to you?' she demanded. 'You look upset.'

'Don't be silly, Mum.' Karen turned and went back into the living-room. 'I – I was surprised to have him come here, that's all.'

Laura took off her coat and hung it in the hall closet before joining her daughter. 'Yes, I suppose it was unexpected,' she conceded. 'Did he want to see your father?'

'I don't think so. In any case, Pop was asleep. He still is, as far as I know.'

Laura nodded, and stood for a moment staring into the fire. 'He doesn't change much, does he? He always was an attractive devil!'

'How should I know?' Karen flung herself on to the couch and picked up a magazine.

Laura looked at her. 'You've seen him before. He spent quite a lot of time with the McMullens when he was at university in Leeds.'

Karen pretended an indifference she didn't feel. 'I don't remember.'

'Oh, yes, you do, Karen.' Laura took a deep breath. 'I happen to know you went out with him.'

Karen's head jerked up. '*Me?*'

'Yes, you, Karen. I know what I'm talking about. There were plenty of people in Wakeley only too willing to tell me that my daughter was getting herself talked

49

about by associating with Howard Whitney's son.'

Karen flung the magazine aside and shrugged helplessly. 'I had no idea!' she exclaimed.

'I know that.'

'Did – did Pop know?' Karen's eyes were wide.

Her mother shook her head. 'No. Do you think if he had, he'd have let it rest there?'

'I suppose not.' Karen got restlessly to her feet. 'Why didn't you tell him? You knew he would have stopped me seeing Alexis?'

'And what good would that have done? You'd have found some way to meet him, if you really wanted to. No, I was quite prepared to wait until you came to your senses, as I was sure you would.'

'But I didn't, did I? Not really. If Daddy hadn't found out where I was going that week-end, I might – well, have gone through with it.'

Laura shrugged. 'If I'd thought there was any danger, then I should have interfered. But quite honestly, you didn't seem particularly sorry when your father prevented you from going.'

'No.' Karen was thoughtful. 'I wasn't. I – I was scared, I guess.' She sighed. 'I've often wondered what Alexis thought when I didn't turn up. That letter I sent was so – so inadequate.'

'Then perhaps it's just as well we sent you to your aunt's in Keswick, isn't it? Thank heaven, you were still at school, and not tied down to some job.'

Karen nodded, thrusting her hands into the pockets of her trousers. 'You must have felt quite perturbed when Daddy told us Alexis was coming back to Wakeley.'

Laura made an indifferent gesture. 'Not particularly. After all, you're older. You've got more sense. And then there's Ray. Not to mention the fact that you're not at all the kind of woman to attract him now. He's used to a much more sophisticated set.'

Karen knew that what her mother was saying was true,

but that didn't prevent a small core of dissatisfaction from spreading through her system. She wondered what her mother would say if she told her that Alexis had asked her to have dinner with him one evening. She had refused that was true, too, but there was a disturbing awareness inside her that the attraction he had held for her seven years ago was not dead.

During the next few days, Karen's father made a slow but steady improvement, although it was obvious it would be several weeks before he could resume working. Both John McMullen and Jim Summerton, the director of the Wakeley branch of Whitney Textiles, called to see him and offer their good wishes for his speedy recovery, and their concern seemed to lighten the burden of his incapacity. His reactions to Alexis Whitney's inquiry were typically brusque.

The weather continued very cold. As it was freezing most of the time, the snow did not have a chance to melt and disappear, and in consequence the moorland slopes on the outskirts of the town became the rendezvous for all kinds of winter sports. Karen and Ray joined the younger members of his family and went tobogganing and she came home flushed and exhilarated after a particularly strenuous evening to find the dark green Aston Martin, which she recognized as belonging to Alexis Whitney, parked outside her house.

Ray frowned as he brought his medium-sized saloon to a halt behind the sports car. 'Visitors?' he asked, in surprise.

Karen sighed. 'I think it's Daddy's boss,' she replied, and then, on impulse, went on: 'Won't you come in for a few minutes? For coffee?'

'It is rather late,' said Ray, glancing at his watch. 'I had some marking to do, actually.'

Karen tugged his arm appealingly. 'Please!'

Ray capitulated. 'Oh, all right. Just for ten minutes,

51

then. But what about your father? Won't he mind when his superior's there?'

Karen pushed open her door and slid out. 'Don't be silly, Ray. You're almost one of the family.'

Ray locked the car. 'Almost, but not quite. Thought any more about what I asked you?'

Karen sighed and tucked her arm through his. 'Of course I have. Just give me a little time, Ray.'

Inside there were voices coming from the living-room, and Karen indicated that Ray should take his coat off while she hung her parka away in the hall closet. Then, summoning all her courage, she opened the living-room door.

Her father and mother were seated in the armchairs on either side of the fireplace, while Alexis was relaxing lazily on the couch. Her father was wearing his dressing-gown, as he had only just begun to get up in the afternoons for a while, and a rug was tucked about his feet.

When Karen entered the room followed closely by Ray, Alexis got immediately to his feet and regarded them with those strange tawny eyes of his. In a cream denim suit with a belted jacket and narrow-fitting trousers he looked lean and powerful, his thick, straight, light hair brushing his collar.

Laura Sinclair rose hastily and interposed herself between Alexis and the two by the door. 'You know my daughter, of course, Mr. Whitney,' she said politely. 'And this is Ray Nichols, her boy-friend.'

Karen cringed at her mother's choice of words. It made her feel young and immature again, a teenager with teenage friends.

Alexis as usual was calm and relaxed. 'How do you do, Mr. Nichols,' he said, shaking Ray's hand with casual ease, and Ray responded automatically. Then his gaze moved on to Karen, making her overwhelmingly conscious of her wind-roughened cheeks and tangled hair. 'Hello again, Miss Sinclair.'

'Hello.' Karen gave an awkward grimace in lieu of a smile, and moved into the room, going to warm her hands unnecessarily at the fire.

'Won't you sit down again, Mr. Whitney?' Laura indicated the couch, but Alexis shook his head.

'I'm afraid I shall have to be going,' he replied apologetically. 'But I'll call again and discuss this when we have more time, Dan.'

Karen's father moved his shoulders irritably. 'I don't see what there is to discuss. It's all been decided, if you ask me.'

Alexis moved towards the door. 'I'll see you later,' he said, and smiling at Laura he went out into the hall.

Karen glanced round as he left the room feeling a momentary pang that he should go without saying any more. But what did she expect him to say? What did she *want* him to say?

The sound of the front door closing behind him brought her father to life. 'I knew it,' he muttered, looking up into Ray's uncomprehending face. 'I knew it. No sooner is he here than he's trying to change the system! My God, I've heard of men being fired because of mechanization, but not because of de-mechanization!'

Laura, coming back into the room at that moment, said: 'They're not being fired, Dan—'

'All right. Being made redundant, then. It amounts to the same thing. They won't have jobs, will they?'

Laura sighed. 'Nothing's been decided yet. You know that.'

'Huh!' Her husband sounded sceptical, and Ray said:

'What's happening? How is he planning to de-mechanize? I thought there was no mechanization in the wool sorting. It's all done by hand, isn't it?'

'The sorting, yes. This is concerned with the conveying of wool from the warehouse to the sorters. At the moment we have a conveyor belt. That's where the mechanization comes in.'

'I see.' Ray sat down by the fire and held out his hands to the flames. 'And you say this chap's going to do away with your conveyor belt system?'

'Well, that's his idea.'

'Why, Pop?' Karen was interested in spite of herself.

Her father frowned at her name for him but didn't refer to it then. Instead he went on: 'At the moment, we have two chaps putting bales of wool on to the conveyor belt in the warehouse. Then there are two more chaps who take it off the belt in the sorting department and distribute it by the means of hand barrows to the individual sorters.'

'That sounds reasonable.' Ray offered Karen's father a cigarette, but he refused.

'It is reasonable. I was there when the conveyor belt was installed.'

'Then what's the problem?' asked Karen, growing impatient.

Her father frowned. 'Whitney thinks it's a waste of manpower. He says one man, with the use of a forklift truck, could do the job more efficiently.'

Ray considered this for a few minutes. 'But wouldn't that slow the job down? I mean, at the moment you can put any number of bales on to the conveyor belt at any one time.'

'My point exactly. Oh, I can see what he's trying to do, of course. It's obvious. His whole objective is to cut the finances of the department to an absolute minimum, and if he can go back to old Howard and tell him how he's saved him half a dozen men's wages, he'll think he's some kind of miracle worker.'

Karen listened in silence. For all she had it from her own father what Alexis was trying to do, she couldn't altogether accept it. She would never have believed him to be a mean man, whatever his faults, and surely he was not small enough as to make men redundant just to ingratiate

54

himself with the accounts department. It didn't altogether add up, but it was not up to her to make that kind of assessment.

Laura, too, seemed to have heard enough. 'Dan Sinclair,' she exclaimed heatedly, 'I am getting heartily sick of hearing you grumbling about that man. If you ask me you're jealous because you didn't get offered the job, and you're finding any reason to be awkward!'

Karen's father had the grace to look slightly subdued. 'You don't understand, Laura—'

'I understand very well. I understand that Karen and Ray have been out since just after seven, and I've no doubt they're dying for some coffee and something to eat. Aren't you, Ray?' She patted his shoulder encouragingly.

'That would be nice,' admitted Ray with a smile, and Karen's father snorted grudgingly.

'Oh, I know, I do go on about it. Anyway, as you say, Laura, nothing's been decided yet. They can't do anything until I'm back in harness.'

Two days later, Shirley Scott, the headmaster's secretary, came to the staff room while Karen and her colleagues were having their morning coffee.

'There's a telephone call for you, Karen,' she said, from the doorway, and Karen who had been standing talking to Stephen Sheridan, the art master, looked round in surprise.

'For me?' she said.

The staff were not encouraged to have personal calls in school hours, and apart from her mother she couldn't think of anyone who might phone her. Perhaps her father had had a relapse.

'It's a man,' remarked Shirley dryly, dispelling this thought, and Karen was aware of Ray watching her as she walked across the room to join the other girl.

As they walked along the corridor Karen said: 'Did he give his name?'

Shirley shook her head. 'No. But he sounds dishy. Did you see Ray's face when I said it was a man?' she giggled.

Karen felt impatient. Impatient with Shirley for deliberately baiting Ray, and impatient with herself for feeling this pulsating sense of excitement invading her system. It had to be Alexis Whitney; who else could it be?

Shirley was tactful enough to leave her alone to take the call in the secretary's office, and Karen lifted the receiver nervously. 'H – hello! Karen Sinclair speaking.'

'Hello, Karen.' His voice was just as attractive over the phone and her palms moistened. 'I hope I've not rung at an inconvenient time.'

'We're not supposed to have private calls in school hours,' replied Karen stiffly.

'I see. Well, I didn't see how else I could get in touch with you. Other than at home, of course, which didn't seem such a good idea.'

'Why did you want to get in touch with me, Mr. Whitney?' Karen managed to maintain a formal tone.

There was a moment's pause, and then he went on: 'I've been invited to a dinner party at the Summertons'. They've asked me to bring a guest. I wondered if you'd like to come.'

Karen sank down weakly into Shirley's chair. That he should think he could simply ring her and invite her out without possessing any right to do so!

'You've got a nerve!' she burst out hotly.

'I know. I've got several.' His tone was mocking.

'You think you can just ring me up and I'll jump at the opportunity, is that it?'

'If you want my honest opinion, I think you'll refuse,' he replied coolly. 'But there's no harm in asking, is there?'

'Why invite me? I shouldn't have thought you'd have had any difficulty in finding someone eager and willing to go out with you.'

'Did I say I had had difficulty?'

'No. But – well, you wouldn't have asked me, unless . . . unless . . .'

'Unless what? Unless there was no one else?' He sounded amused. 'Just for your information, I haven't asked anyone else – yet.'

'I don't believe you.'

'I don't lie.' His tone had hardened slightly, and she felt a momentary regret.

'Well, anyway, I'm sorry . . .'

'You're not coming?'

'No.'

'Right.' There was a short pause. 'Be seeing you—'

'Wait! Wait a minute!' Ever afterwards Karen could not explain what it was that made her say that. But she had arrested his attention, and he said, rather shortly:

'Yes? What is it?'

Karen sought about for words, ignoring her conscience which was appalled at this unexpected turn of events. 'I – I – when is this dinner party?'

'Tomorrow evening.'

'Oh! Friday.' Karen wet her dry lips with her tongue. On Fridays she usually stayed in. Ray had his choir practice at the school and then went on down to his club for a few drinks with his colleagues.

'Yes, Friday.' Alexis was beginning to sound bored with the whole proceedings.

Karen ran her finger round the mouthpiece of the receiver. 'Will John McMullen be there?'

'I shouldn't think so. Why? Do I take it you're changing your mind?'

Karen was glad he could not see her embarrassment. 'And if I did? Would you mind?'

He uttered an exclamation. 'Are you coming, or are you not?'

Karen hesitated, and then she took the plunge. 'I'll come.'

'Fine. I'll pick you up about seven—'

'No!' Karen was anxious. 'No, don't do that. I'll – I'll meet you. In the High Street.'

'I see. This is to be a secret assignation.' His voice was cool.

'I think it would be better not to antagonize my father at this time,' she answered carefully.

There was silence for a moment and then he sighed. 'Very well. Outside the George Hotel at seven.'

'All right.' Karen swallowed hard. ' 'Bye!'

He did not reply, but she heard his receiver click back on to its rest and she replaced hers slowly. She was committed; and while given the same circumstances she would probably have done the same thing, that didn't stop her from feeling nervous.

The ringing of a bell indicated that breaktime was over and before Karen could gather her scattered composure Shirley came breezing back into the room.

'Come on!' she said. 'Everyone's gone back to their classrooms but you.'

Karen got to her feet, her manner rather absent, and Shirley regarded her critically. 'Who was it?' she asked without ceremony. 'Ray was dying to know.'

Karen heaved a sigh. 'Oh, just my cousin,' she answered, walking towards the door.

'Hmm.' Shirley sounded sceptical. 'You don't look as though you've been talking to your cousin. You look sort of – well, dreamy.'

That was enough to bring Karen to her senses. 'Don't be silly! Dreamy indeed! I was thinking, that's all.'

'Well, you'd better have your explanations prepared before Ray sees you at lunchtime,' remarked Shirley, with annoying perspicacity. 'I don't somehow think he's going to be as easily put off as me!'

CHAPTER FOUR

KAREN had lunch with Ray in the staff canteen, and just as Shirley had warned, he was most inquisitive about her unexpected phone call.

'It was just my cousin Bryan from Keswick,' she exclaimed, disgusted with her own capacity for lying.

'What was he ringing you for?' Ray poured salt on to the side of his plate.

Karen hesitated. 'Oh, he wondered whether I'd like to go over there for the week-end. He – he'd tried to ring me at home last night but couldn't get through, and as it's Thursday already . . .' She shrugged.

'And what did you say?'

'I said I couldn't manage it.'

'We could have gone. On Saturday. We could have stayed overnight and come back Sunday. It would have been a break.'

Karen pushed her potatoes and turnip round her plate. She didn't feel much like eating, but she had to look as though she was enjoying it. 'You know Bryan. He would have expected me to go alone.'

'Well, what of it? Just because he's fond of you it doesn't mean that you have to pander to it.'

'I don't. But anyway, it doesn't matter, does it? Because I'm not going either way.'

Ray grunted. 'The sooner you decide to get engaged to me the better. Then people will know where we stand. You won't constantly have to explain that you're not free any longer.'

'Yes.'

Karen managed a smile and to her relief the subject was dropped. But that didn't stop her from feeling on edge for the rest of the day in case Ray inadvertently mentioned it to her parents.

On Friday afternoon, Karen hurried home from school to wash her hair. She was drying it in front of the fire when her mother returned from a shopping expedition. She raised her eyebrows when she saw Karen, and said: 'You're early, aren't you? What's the panic?'

Karen was glad of the heat of the fire to hide her embarrassment. 'No panic, Mum. But I've promised to go to that new disco with Melanie, and I wanted to wash my hair.' She was almost shocked by her own deviousness, but she had to have a reason to wear a long dress or her parents would be suspicious.

Even so, her mother looked disapproving. 'Does Ray know you're planning to go out with Melanie?'

Karen sighed. 'Does it matter?'

'I think so. I don't think he'd like you to go to a discotheque without him.'

'He's not my keeper, Mum.'

'I know that. But it's obvious he's serious about you, and I don't think you should do anything to hurt him.'

Karen knelt before the fire, combing her fingers through her hair. She knew her mother was right and she was only courting trouble by going out with Alexis Whitney, but that didn't stop her from wanting to go.

'I haven't promised to marry Ray or anything,' she exclaimed.

'Not for the want of asking, I'm sure,' retorted Laura tartly. 'Karen, there are times when you infuriate me! You're twenty-four, you know, not a teenager any longer. Don't you want to get married?'

Karen glanced round. 'I think so. But not just because it's expedient to do so.'

'What do you mean? Ray's a nice boy. Attractive, too, and he comes from a decent family.'

'I just want to be absolutely certain I'm doing the right thing,' Karen persisted. 'Sometimes I'm not sure about Ray. I mean – well – he's not very – demonstrative.'

'If you mean he doesn't indulge in careless petting, then I should think that's all to the good. He respects you. He doesn't go off to discotheques with his pals behind your back.'

Karen turned back to the fire, and did not reply, and eventually her mother took herself off to the kitchen to prepare the evening meal. Realizing she was expected to eat out, Karen scrambled to her feet.

'Oh, by the way, don't make anything for me,' she said. 'I – er – Melanie and I are going to eat at the Chinese before going on to the disco.'

Laura accepted this without question. Karen often ate out with Ray. All the same, Karen's nerves were back on edge again, and she couldn't wait to get away from the house and be free of all this deception.

She wore a long black velvet dress she had had for some time and which she had seldom had occasion to wear. It complemented the pink and white quality of her skin, and with her raven black hair swinging silkily about her shoulders, she looked quite startlingly attractive. Her only jewellery was a pair of huge silver hoops which she wore in her ears and which showed glintingly through the darkness of her hair.

She hadn't an evening coat, but she did have a maxi-length cape in dark green which looked almost as good. She came downstairs wearing the cape, hoping no one would notice the dress beneath, but her mother did.

'Isn't that rather good to wear to a discotheque?' she inquired, with raised eyebrows.

Karen shrugged. 'I never seem to get a chance to wear it. I thought it would make a change.'

Her mother made an indifferent gesture while her father looked up from his newspaper. 'I think she looks very nice,' he said, surprising them both. 'Where's Ray taking you?'

Karen coloured and looked towards her mother helplessly. 'Ray's taking her nowhere,' she said, ignoring her daughter's appealing gaze. 'She's going out with Melanie Trafford.'

But to Karen's relief, her father merely shrugged. 'Oh, well, enjoy yourself.'

Karen thanked him, and with another appealing glance towards her mother she went to the front door. But as she walked the short distance to the High Street she couldn't help feeling terribly guilty. She had only ever deceived her parents once before in her life, and the reasons in both cases were the same.

She reached the George Hotel at one minute past seven, but there was no sign of the green Aston Martin. She looked round uneasily, hoping no one she knew would come along to recognize her, and then almost jumped out of her skin when a voice right behind her said: 'So you made it.'

She swung round and found Alexis regarding her musingly, tall and attractive in a dark overcoat, his hands thrust deep into the pockets.

'I – I was looking for the car,' she said, as his gaze slid over her.

'There are parking restrictions,' he observed dryly. 'It's just round here.'

Karen accompanied him round a corner into a side street and they stopped beside the sleek green sports limousine. It was the first time she had ever been in an Aston Martin; seven years ago he had had an old souped-up M.G.

Alexis put her into the car, and then walked round the bonnet and got in beside her. Flicking the ignition, he said: 'What made you change your mind?'

Karen sought about for a suitable reply. 'Perhaps I thought you wouldn't go through with it,' she murmured insinuatively.

He glanced her way. 'Why?'

'Well – taking me to Mr. Summerton's house. He might not like it.'

Alexis swung the powerful car out into the main road. 'Why should Jim Summerton's likes and dislikes concern me?'

Karen bent her head. 'You know what I mean.'

'Oh, yes. What you mean is, will Jim Summerton tell your father that you were a guest in his house,' remarked Alexis sardonically.

'Well? Will he?'

'Not if I ask him not to. But Jim Summerton won't be the only one there, you know.'

'I'm not likely to know anyone else, am I?'

'I don't know.' Alexis shrugged. 'Maybe – maybe not.'

'You're being deliberately provocative,' she exclaimed.

'And you're being childish,' he returned, stopping at some traffic lights. 'I should have thought by now you'd have been mature enough to choose your own associates without resorting to deceit.'

Karen's face burned. 'It's not as simple as that.'

'Why? Because of your father?'

'Partly.'

'And what's the rest?' The car moved smoothly forward taking the incline towards Moorcourt, the more select part of Wakeley. 'Is it this man Nichols?'

Karen looked through the car's windows. 'I suppose so.'

'You don't wear a ring. You're not engaged, are you?'

'No.'

Alexis shook his head impatiently. 'Then where's the problem?'

'You don't understand. Wakeley isn't like London.'

'What's that supposed to mean?'

'Ray and I have been going out together for more than a year.'

'Have you?' His glance licked over her insolently. 'I never would have guessed.'

63

'I don't understand you.' Karen was frustrated.

'Don't you?' A flicker of amusement crossed his face. 'No? Then perhaps you should.'

Suddenly Karen knew what he meant and she hated him for his cool contempt. 'Going to bed together need not necessarily form part of the relationship between a man and a woman,' she snapped. 'Don't judge everyone by your own standards!'

He smiled. 'Obviously that's a raw point with you.'

Karen seethed. 'It is not a raw point! As I said before, Wakeley is not like London. Here we have respect for one another.'

'Oh! Is that what it is?' He was mocking her, and all of a sudden she wished she had not agreed to come. 'Incredible!' he went on, turning the car between stone gateposts and driving up a short slope to a rambling old house with light spilling from most of the windows. 'You're just as – old-fashioned now as you were seven years ago. I can hardly believe it.'

He brought the car to a halt and Karen sat mutinously in her seat, wondering whether she dare demand that he drive her home again. But he had got out and walked round the vehicle, and presently he swung open her door and looked down at her lazily.

'Are you going to stay there all evening?'

'I wish I could!' Karen's fingers curled inside her cape.

'Why? Have I hurt your feelings?' She had the distinct feeling he was laughing at her. 'All right, I apologize if I've offended you – if I've shown – *disrespect*!'

Now she was sure he was amusing himself at her expense, and she clenched her fists angrily. 'I want to go home!'

'Do you?' Alexis's expression hardened slightly. 'Well, I'm afraid that's out of the question.'

She looked up at him. 'Why? Why is it? I don't know why you brought me here. You obviously find me very amusing.'

'Perhaps that's why,' he replied, and she didn't know whether he was serious or otherwise.

Realizing he was not about to give in to her and take her home, Karen pushed her legs out of the car and stood up. Alexis closed the door behind her and then indicated that she should precede him up the steps to the door. A uniformed maid admitted them, and they entered an old oak-panelled hall, warmly carpeted in shades of red and orange.

The maid offered to take their coats and Karen unfastened her cape reluctantly. Although the black dress had long sleeves, it had a low round neckline that showed off her skin to advantage, and she was self-consciously aware of Alexis watching her. He was not wearing a dinner jacket but a dark blue suit with pale blue shirt and tie, and the darkness of the material accentuated the silvery lightness of his hair and the deep tan of his skin.

Although Alexis appraised her appearance thoroughly he did not have time to say anything before a door to the side of the hall opened and a man came to greet them. From the room behind him there drifted the sound of voices and laughter, and Karen quivered in anticipation.

Jim Summerton was a stocky man of medium height. Karen didn't know him very well, although she had met him from time to time, most recently when he came to the house to see her father. Her impressions of him, coloured by her father's opinion, had been of a rather stern Scotsman, without much sense of humour, but this evening he seemed entirely different.

'Alexis!' he exclaimed warmly, crossing the hall to them and shaking hands. 'Glad you could come! Hello, Karen! How are you? How's that father of yours getting on?'

Karen responded politely and then their host interposed himself between them and led them across to the opened door of the lounge where his other guests were

65

having cocktails before dinner. To Karen's relief there were only five other guests apart from Alexis and herself, and she knew none of them personally. There was Jim Summerton's wife Mary, of course, and Lucy, his daughter, but Karen didn't know them particularly well either. She was introduced to the other guests: to Frank and Winifred Perry, who farmed just outside of Wakeley, to George and Sylvia Horner, whom Karen recognized by their name as being the owners of Streatham Grange, a large riding school on the outskirts of Wakeley, and to the Horners' son, Michael, who was in his late teens. They seemed a friendly group, although Karen sensed a certain speculation about her presence there, and she wondered whether indeed Alexis had been expected to bring a guest. Maybe it was accepted because he was who he was, and she might conceivably be the latest in a long line of conquests. She found the idea did not appeal to her, and she began to appreciate the invidiousness of her position.

However, it soon became apparent that Lucy Summerton, at least, considered that Alexis's presence at the dinner party was solely her concern, and as Karen and Alexis were separated at the outset, Karen soon found herself left in the hands of young Michael Horner. So much so that she actually began to wonder whether she had not just been invited to make up the numbers. Whenever she looked in Alexis's direction, he seemed absorbed with what Lucy and her parents were saying to him, and Karen couldn't dispel the surge of jealousy that enveloped her no matter how she tried.

Not that Lucy Summerton was a particularly beautiful girl. She had a rather attractive face and a rounded figure, it was true, but it was the elegance of her clothes and the artistry of her hairdresser who really were responsible for her sophisticated appearance.

After a couple of drinks, during which time Sylvia Horner questioned Karen extensively about her work at the comprehensive school, they all went in to dinner, and she found herself seated between Michael and Frank Perry on one side of the long polished table, while Alexis was seated with Lucy and the Horners at the other.

The meal, delicious though it was, seemed endless, and Karen had to force herself not to watch Alexis across the table or to try and listen to his conversation. Michael was charming to her, although she found his conversation a little immature, and after a few drinks Frank Perry unbent sufficiently to ask her whether she did much riding. As Karen had only ridden in the environs of a riding school as a child, her reply was not what he had expected, and he was silent for a while before going on to tell her that he loved hunting and that he had been blooded when he was only five years old. As Karen was opposed to fox-hunting as a sport, and considered blooding a child as being one of the most barbarous acts she had ever heard of, this provoked a lively argument, and she found herself the cynosure of all eyes. However, far from becoming angry with her, Frank Perry seemed to find her views refreshing, and when they returned to the lounge for coffee he seated himself beside her, much to his wife's chagrin, and proceeded to tell her all about himself. A man in his forties, he was a typical countryman, and he knew all there was to know about farming. It was only when he began showing an interest in her affairs that Karen felt any sense of withdrawal, and realized that he might conceivably get the wrong idea about her.

Conversation became general, and as Jim Summerton ensured that no one's glass was ever empty, there was a comfortable air of conviviality about the proceedings. Alexis was seated across the room from Karen with George Horner, while Lucy was perched on the arm of his chair, but from time to time she sensed his eyes upon her.

Once she glanced at her watch and discovered it was already after ten o'clock, which surprised her somewhat.

The last couple of hours seemed to have gone by so quickly, and she wondered how soon the party would break up. The disco would be closing at ten-thirty, and her parents would expect her home soon after eleven.

At a quarter to eleven, Mary Summerton suggested coffee and everyone agreed except Karen, who now looked deliberately across at Alexis, trying to convey her anxiety. He seemed to sense her unease and rising abruptly to his feet, he said: 'I'm afraid we'll have to be going, Mary. Karen's a working girl, you know, and it's getting late.'

Lucy looked annoyed. 'It is Saturday tomorrow,' she pointed out.

Alexis smiled down at her petulant features. 'So it is. Never mind. It's time we were leaving.'

'Are you sure, Karen?' Mary Summerton was basically a kind woman. 'I'm sure if you telephoned your parents—'

'No – really.' Karen stood up too. 'I – thank you for a lovely evening.'

Mary smiled. 'You must get Alexis to bring you again.'

'Yes.' Karen was doubtful, aware of Lucy's irritation.

Gradually they made their way out into the hall, making casual farewells, Alexis promising to phone the Horners. The maid brought their outdoor things and presently Alexis was dropping her cape about her shoulders.

The Aston Martin was cold, and the windscreen was filmed with ice until he sprayed it with some kind of defrosting liquid. Then he got into the car beside her and started the engine which fired without hesitation.

'You – you can drop me in the High Street again,' murmured Karen awkwardly, as they drove down Moorcourt.

'No!' said Alexis distinctly, and then indicated a building on their left. 'That's where I live. Have you ever been there?'

'If you mean when Mr. Pierce lived there, no. And what do you mean, you won't drop me in the High Street?'

'Just that. I don't intend to leave you in the middle of Wakeley at this time of night to walk home alone. It would be crazy! If anyone sees you with me, then it's just too bad.'

Karen sighed. 'And of course someone will.'

'Well, what of it? Don't take life so seriously. What have we done this evening that you couldn't tell your parents about?'

'Absolutely nothing,' said Karen, her tone rather flat, but quite honestly that was how she was feeling.

Alexis looked at her strangely. 'Do I detect a note of dissatisfaction in your voice?'

'Don't be ridiculous!' Karen looked impatiently through the windows. 'It's beginning to snow again.'

'Yes.' He sounded thoughtful. 'And I have to go to London in the morning.'

Karen looked his way. 'You're driving down?'

'No. I shall take the train from Leeds.' They were approaching the traffic lights again and he slowed almost to a halt. 'Tell me something, Karen, why did you agree to come out with me this evening?'

She moved restlessly in her seat. 'I – I thought it would be something – different.'

'Do you mean – diverting?'

She frowned. 'Need we have a post-mortem?'

'Yes, I think we need.' Alexis pulled on his handbrake even though the lights had changed to green. 'Why – if you're going to marry this man Nichols – did you run the risk of making him jealous by coming out with me?'

Karen shrugged. 'Like you said – for old times' sake.'

'Really?' He was half turned in his seat towards her, his arm along the back of hers, and she was intensely conscious of the cool appraisal of those strange amber eyes. The traffic lights were in the centre of Wakeley and she glanced round helplessly, sure someone was about to come along and recognize her.

Breathing quickly, she said: 'What do you want me to say? I – I suppose I was – flattered.'

Thick lashes narrowed his eyes. 'Flattered?' He frowned. 'I see.'

'Now will you take me home?' Karen glanced at her watch. 'It's nearly half past eleven. My parents will be worried about me.'

He picked up a strand of her night-dark hair and played with it absently, smoothing the threads across his fingers. 'Surely they've no need to be worried about a girl like you,' he remarked lazily. 'Not someone with such pure ideals.'

Karen sighed. 'Please,' she said.

Alexis's eyes flickered over her, resting for a disturbing moment on her mouth and she almost felt as though he had touched her. Then, with a shrug, he swung round in his seat and releasing the handbrake the car rolled smoothly forward.

It only took another couple of minutes to reach Karen's home and the Aston Martin came to a noiseless halt at the end of their short drive.

'Thank you.'

Karen reached for the door handle, but Alexis forestalled her, reaching past her to secure it for a moment longer. 'Aren't you going to kiss me?' he inquired softly. 'Er – for old times' sake, of course.'

Karen was very close to him now. He was deliberately imprisoning her with his arm and his face was only inches from hers. In the gloom she couldn't read his expression, but she didn't need any illumination to be aware of the lean strength of his body or the clean male smell about him. She had visions of her mother at the window, seeing the car, recognizing it, wondering why Karen didn't get out.

'Why are you doing this?' she demanded tremulously.

'You're not interested in me.'

'Make me – interested, I mean.'

Karen gasped. 'No!'

'All right, I'll have to do it myself, then,' he said, and sliding his hand under her hair he gripped the back of her neck, turning her face towards him.

Karen didn't struggle. It would have been futile to do so considering his superior strength. But when his mouth covered hers she pressed her lips together tightly and refused to respond.

He lifted his head slightly and she was aware of the questioning penetration of his gaze. Then he kissed the curve of her chin, the hollows of her cheeks, the corner of her ear, catching the lobe between his teeth and biting gently.

When Karen thought he was about to seek her mouth again he suddenly drew back, releasing her abruptly. 'Good night,' he said coolly, drawing on his driving gloves.

Karen gave him a startled glance. She felt curiously bereft and hopelessly out of her depth.

'G – good night,' she stammered, and thrust open the door. She scarcely had time to slam it again before the powerful car drove away.

CHAPTER FIVE

The fact that neither of her parents was up when she got in was almost an anticlimax, and Karen felt absurdly near to tears. It was a long time since she had cried about anything, and she didn't altogether know why she felt like crying now. But she did!

The week-end was quiet. She spent Saturday afternoon and evening at the home of Ray' parents, and on Sunday the weather was so bad that they didn't meet until the evening and then only to go to the cinema.

Karen was glad when Monday came round. It was good to get back to school and back to work. When she was at home she had too much time to think, and she had done a lot of thinking over the week-end.

One thing had clarified itself, however. The silly emotional feelings she had cherished about Alexis Whitney all these years had been nothing but the result of an overcharged imagination. She was glad she had not responded to him. How galling it must have been for him to discover that in one respect at least she had grown up!

A week later she ran into Lucy Summerton in the supermarket.

The other girl was wandering around aimlessly while Karen was busily collecting some things for her mother in her lunch break. Lucy looked slim and attractive in a sleek brown trouser suit, while Karen was self-consciously aware of the limitations of her fur-lined, hooded poplin mackintosh.

To her surprise, Lucy seemed pleased to see her, and joining the queue at the checkout behind Karen, she said: 'How are you?' in quite friendly tones.

Karen was not one to bear a grudge and with a smile

she answered: 'Fine, thanks. Isn't the weather appalling?'

'Yes.' Lucy looked beyond her to the slush-covered pavements outside the supermarket windows. 'You look flustered. Are you in a hurry?'

'Well, not exactly now,' admitted Karen ruefully. 'I was, but I think I've got everything. My mother asked me to get a few things to save her having to come out.'

'I see.' Lucy nodded. 'What time do you have to be back at school?'

Karen reached the checkout and began unloading her things on to the counter. 'Oh, about a quarter to two,' she said, fumbling in her shopping-bag for her purse.

Lucy frowned. 'Then you've time for a coffee. There's a bar next door, and I'm sure you could do with a few moments' rest before you get back to the grind.'

Karen hesitated. Her first instincts were to refuse, but for those very reasons she thought again. By avoiding speaking to Lucy Summerton she was admitting to an awareness of her involvement with Alexis, and it surely didn't matter to her whether he was involved or not.

Taking a deep breath, she nodded, and said: 'Thank you. I'd like that.'

Once ensconced on a low banquette in the discreetly-lit coffee bar next door, Karen began to have second thoughts. While Lucy went for their coffees, Karen had refused anything to eat, she began to wonder exactly why Lucy should have taken the trouble to invite her at all. After all, they had very little, if anything, in common, and ten days ago it had been obvious that she had resented Karen accompanying Alexis to her home.

Lucy returned, and slid on to the banquette opposite, pushing a cup of creamy liquid towards her. 'Hmm,' she said, her eyes flickering over Karen's white blouse and navy cardigan. 'This is nice, isn't it?'

Karen smiled. There wasn't a lot she could say. Seeking about for a safe topic, she sipped her coffee, and wished

73

situations did not so easily react upon her.

Lucy seemed to have no such anxieties. Her motives for bringing Karen here were soon made clear. She wanted to talk about Alexis Whitney.

'Tell me,' she said, 'have you known Alexis very long?'

That was a difficult question and Karen wasn't at all sure how to answer it. At last she decided to be truthful, and said: 'Actually I met him seven years ago. When he was at university in Leeds. We met at a party given by some mutual friends.'

'Oh, I see.' Lucy seemed to find this eminently satisfying and Karen wondered whether this was because she had previously imagined that their relationship had developed remarkably quickly in the few weeks Alexis had been in Wakely. 'So you'll be quite old friends.'

Karen shrugged. 'Sort of.'

'Was that before or after his father married again?'

Karen shook her head. 'I don't know. I didn't know him that well.'

'No, of course not.' Lucy sipped her coffee in a rather satisfied way. She raised her delicately plucked eyebrows and went on: 'That was all rather – unpleasant, wasn't it?'

'What was?' Karen was out of her depth now.

'Why, Alexis's father getting married again, of course.'

'I don't know anything about it. Why shouldn't he get married again if he wants to? It's quite a common occurrence, isn't it?'

'Oh, yes, but this was something else.' Lucy lay back in her seat and opened the expensive suède handbag that lay on the table between them. 'Cigarette?' Karen shook her head and she extracted one of the long American cigarettes and placed it between her lips, lighting it with a gold lighter. Then she went on: 'Alexis's mother had only been dead a little over six months when it happened.'

74

Karen moved uncomfortably. She didn't particularly want to hear the personal details of Alexis's father's life and she couldn't yet understand why Lucy should be regaling her with them. 'I don't think it's anything to do with me,' she began, but Lucy ignored her.

'The most sordid part of all was that Michelle, the young woman Howard Whitney married, had been going about with his son for the best part of a year!'

Karen felt an unpleasant sensation in her stomach. 'I expect these things happen sometimes,' she managed.

'Oh, yes.' Lucy blew smoke into the air above their heads. 'Oh, yes. But you see Michelle knew that Alexis would never marry her, so rather than forgo the Whitney millions, she made a deliberate play for his father.' Lucy shook her head, a sardonic expression marring her face. 'I think she had some quaint idea of capturing two birds with one stone, but it didn't quite work out like that.'

'I don't see why you're telling me all this,' remarked Karen carefully, running her finger round the rim of her cup.

'I thought you'd be interested,' Lucy shrugged. 'Women have always been interested in Alexis. I've known him since we were children, and even in those days ...' Her voice trailed away insinuatively. 'Naturally, being the son of a millionaire makes one terribly eligible, but it's not just that with Alexis, is it? I mean, I'd want him even if he hadn't a sou!'

Karen finished her coffee rather quickly. Now she understood. She wasn't exactly being warned off Alexis, although there was an air of possessiveness in Lucy's voice when she spoke of him; but rather she was being informed, very politely, that any aspirations she might have in that direction were all right so long as she didn't expect marriage as part of the bargain.

Having got that off her chest, Lucy changed the subject completely and began asking Karen about her school work, showing an assumed interest in methods of education today as compared to several years ago.

But Karen was no longer in a mood for casual conversation, and as soon as she reasonably could she rose to her feet. 'I must be going,' she said, her voice rather tight. 'Thank you for the coffee – and the conversation.'

Lucy made no effort to detain her. 'Good-bye, Karen,' she responded easily. 'I expect we'll run into one another again some time.'

Not if I have anything to do with it, thought Karen to herself bitterly, and with a faint smile marched to the door and went out. Even the smell of exhaust fumes and the icy chill of the air was preferable to the expensive aroma of Lucy's perfume.

The following week her father returned to work, and he came home on his first evening grumbling that in his absence Ian Halliday had been allowed to do his job.

'Bloody insolence!' he muttered. 'Trying to make out I'm not needed – that Halliday can take my place at any time!'

Laura set a steaming steak and kidney pudding down on the table and gave him a wry smile. 'Made a mess, has he?'

Her husband fidgeted irritably with his knife and fork. 'I didn't say that exactly.'

'What Pop means is that Ian's coped admirably in his absence,' remarked Karen, with an attempt at facetiousness.

Her father gave her a quelling look. 'I didn't mean any such thing! He's done well enough, I suppose, but he doesn't work as I do. It will take me weeks to get back into the swing of things again.'

'Well, what do you normally do if you're off?' asked Laura.

'When Jeff was there, he used to keep my work in order,' retorted her husband. 'But Whitney's given young Ian a free hand, if you ask me.'

'Surely that's reasonable!' exclaimed Karen, in spite of her intention to remain silent. 'He's got to learn somehow.'

'Leave it, Karen.' Her mother looked at her exasperatedly. 'And you too, Dan. Heavens, it's been marvellous these past weeks that you've been off work. I've not heard a thing about lost bales of Australian fleece or blend sheets that won't add up! Let's keep it that way, shall we?'

Karen's father shrugged, and set about carving the steak and kidney pie. The subject was dropped and yet Karen thought it was just another example of how, since his return to Wakeley, Alexis Whitney had invaded their lives.

On Thursday evening, Karen was walking out of school as usual, with Ray, when the man who seemed to be occupying such a lot of her thoughts lately stepped out of the shadows to confront them. In the light that spilled from the wide porch he looked disturbingly attractive, a thick cream anorak and denim trousers accentuating the lean length of his legs. He gave Ray a casual word of greeting and then turned to Karen.

'Your father's working late this evening. He tried to ring your mother, but apparently the phone's out of order. In any event, I was coming this way, so I offered to let you know.'

Karen was taken aback. 'Well, thank you.' She glanced awkwardly at Ray. 'I – I hope you haven't had to wait long.'

'No. I've only just arrived. I was about to come inside looking for you.' Alexis was faintly smiling, and she wondered why. He looked at Ray. 'Just on your way home?'

It was an attempt at dismissal and Ray looked indignantly at Karen, waiting for her to explain.

'Oh – Ray always runs me home,' she said hastily. 'I

77

don't have any transport, you see.'

Alexis looked down at the pile of books in her arms. 'You live near Karen, do you, Mr. Nichols?'

'Not particularly.' Karen could tell that Ray was resenting being questioned like this. 'But I always see her safely home.'

Alexis nodded. 'I see. Well, I'll save you the trouble this evening. I'm going in her direction myself.'

Karen shivered, as much with expectation as cold, but Ray seemed to take it as an indication that she was tired of standing talking. Turning to her, he said: 'Is that all right with you, Karen?' in a stiff voice.

Karen sighed. 'I expect so,' she replied unhappily. After all, what else could she say?

Ray shrugged. 'Okay. Then I'll be getting along. Will I see you later?'

'Of course you will.' Karen touched his arm appealingly. 'You're coming round, aren't you?'

'Very well.' Ray tucked up the collar of his coat. 'Good night – Mr. Whitney. See you about eight, Karen.'

'Fine.' Karen smiled encouragingly, and watched as he made his way across the quadrangle to where the teachers parked their cars. Then she turned to Alexis. 'Shall we go?'

Alexis nodded lazily, and lifted the pile of exercise books out of her arms. 'Come on,' he said, offering her his free hand. 'It's rather slippery, so be careful.'

Karen hesitated only a moment before reluctantly putting her hand into his. She was wearing gloves, but he was not, and his fingers closed firmly round hers.

'Hi, Karen! Are you waiting for Ray? I think he's gone.'

The light but inquisitive tones arrested them, and Karen turned unwillingly to face Shirley Scott. 'Hello, Shirley! Yes, Ray has gone. He left a few minutes ago.'

'Oh, I see. What a pity!' Shirley's observant gaze missed nothing. 'I was going to ask him for a lift.'

Ignoring Karen's surreptitious attempts to extract her hand from his, Alexis said: 'Can we give you a lift?'

Shirley dimpled, 'That's very kind of you. Are you going into Wakeley?'

'We can do.' Alexis was urbane.

'Well, fine!' Shirley fell into step beside them. 'Er – are you Karen's cousin, by any chance?'

Karen couldn't look at Alexis, but he seemed unconcerned. 'No. Why? Do I look like her cousin?'

Shirley giggled. 'I don't even know her cousin,' she admitted. 'It's just your voice – it's similar.' She glanced at the girl by her side. 'Isn't it, Karen?'

Karen shrugged. 'Perhaps.'

'You're a teacher, Miss – Miss—' Alexis paused.

'Scott. Shirley Scott.' She gave Karen another determined stare. 'No, I'm not a teacher. I'm secretary to the head.'

'Oh, I see.' Alexis inclined his head. 'I suppose that's an interesting occupation.'

'Well, it is. But I'm always open to offers!' Shirley giggled again, and Karen was furious with herself for the surge of jealousy that was sweeping over her. What was the matter with her? She ought to know what Alexis was like by now. And Shirley, too, for that matter . . .

They reached the Aston Martin and while Alexis unlocked the doors Shirley stood admiring its sleek lines. 'Will you get in the back, Karen?' he suggested, tipping forward his seat. 'Then – Miss Scott can get out more easily.'

'Of course.'

Karen was curt, but she couldn't help it. Alexis had put the pile of exercise books on the back seat and as she stumbled getting in, she upset them and they tumbled all about the floor. Cursing silently to herself, she began picking them up again while Shirley got in, and refused to be placated by the other girl's conspiratorial wink.

'Karen didn't tell me your name,' remarked Shirley, as

the powerful car nosed out of the school gates and on to the road.

'Whitney,' supplied Alexis briefly. 'Alexis Whitney.'

'Oh, then you're – that is – doesn't your father own the mill?'

'That's right.' Alexis accelerated away. 'Where can I drop you?'

Shirley looked about her. 'Anywhere near the centre, please. Wherever it's easiest for you to park.'

Alexis stopped in the High Street and Shirley gave him a beaming smile. 'Thanks very much. This is marvellous!'

'That's all right.' Alexis was deprecatory.

Shirley thrust open the door and got out, then she turned and waved at them both before walking away. Alexis turned to Karen.

'You can get in the front now,' he said.

'Thank you. I'll stay in the back,' she retorted, preventing the exercise books from sliding around with her arm.

Alexis regarded her for a moment longer, and then with a shrug he put the car into gear and they swept forward, past where Shirley was waiting to cross the road. She raised her hand, and Alexis acknowledged it with a movement of his head.

But to Karen's surprise he did not take the next turning for Norfolk Road which led to her parents' house. Instead, he drove on past the George Hotel and up the road towards Moorcourt.

Leaning forward, she said: 'Where do you think you're going?'

'We're going to my house,' he remarked calmly. 'For a drink. Then I'll take you home.'

Karen seethed, 'I don't want to go to your house.'

'That's too bad. Because we're there.'

The Aston Martin turned between stone gateposts, similar to those outside the Summerton house some distance up the road, and came to a halt at the foot of shallow stone steps.

Alexis thrust open his door and slid out, and then leaned in to hold forward his seat so that she could get out, too. She considered refusing, but that would have been childish, so with ill-grace she scrambled out. Alexis slammed shut the door and stood looking down at her for a moment.

'Don't look so cross,' he said mockingly. 'Blake will think I've abducted you.'

'Blake?' Karen frowned.

'My man. I can't exactly say what his title should be. He seems capable of doing anything and everything.'

'Oh. I see.' Karen looked up at the grey stone façade of the house. Then she returned her attention to the man at her side. 'And what about my mother? I thought the idea was to let her know that my father is working late.'

'There's plenty of time.' Alexis put his hand beneath her elbow. 'Come on! I'm sure you could use a drink. It's too cold to stand about out here.'

They entered a panelled hall, again similar in design to that of the Summertons, but the furnishings were different, of course. A stocky little man came to greet them, and he looked questioningly at Karen as he welcomed Alexis.

'Allow me to introduce you to Blake,' remarked Alexis lazily. 'Blake, this is Miss Sinclair.'

'How do you do, miss.' Blake helped her off with her coat. 'My, isn't it a cold evening?'

Karen smiled, appreciating the warmth of the central heating system. 'It *is* rather.'

Alexis dropped his anorak over the banister. 'Have there been any calls?'

'Only one, sir. From Mr. Howard. He tried to reach you at the mill and couldn't. He asked if you'd ring him back later.'

Alexis nodded. 'All right. Thanks.'

'Will Miss Sinclair be staying to dinner, sir?'

'I'm afraid not.' Alexis considered his guest thoughtfully. Flicking back the cuff of his dark green knitted shirt, he consulted his wrist watch. 'I'll eat about seven, if that's suitable.'

'Yes, sir.'

Alexis signified his dismissal, and then led Karen across the softly carpeted hall and into a room on their right. It was an attractively furnished study, the walls partially book-lined and partially panelled. There was an olive green carpet on the floor, and long curtains of darker green and amber. A huge mahogany desk stood square in the centre of the room with buttoned leather armchairs on either side.

Alexis closed the door and then indicated one of the soft leather chairs. 'Sit down. Relax. What would you like to drink? Martini, sherry – or something stronger?'

Karen made a careless gesture. 'Oh, sherry will do.'

Alexis made no demur and crossing to a polished cabinet slid it wide to reveal a comprehensive array of alcohol. As he poured her sherry Karen found herself watching him, realizing that the close-fitting denim trousers were hardly the sort of thing he would wear to the office, even allowing for the fact that that office was in a woollen mill. With sudden intuition, she said: 'Have you been to work this afternoon?'

Alexis came across with her sherry and handed it to her. 'That's a strange question,' he commented, turning back to pour himself some whisky.

Karen frowned into her drink. 'Well? Have you?'

Alexis swallowed half his whisky at a gulp. 'I was in the office approximately an hour ago,' he replied.

'Oh.' She felt rather deflated. Then her eyes strayed over him again, noticing that he had unfastened the neck of his shirt and that the brown skin of his throat was just visible. 'Do you normally go to the office dressed – well, dressed like that?'

Alexis gave her a tolerant smile. 'Is something wrong with what I'm wearing?'

'No. No, you know what I mean.' Karen sighed.

'All right. I'll be honest and admit that my visit was a fleeting one. I've spent the day with Will Saunders, the wool buyer, at a rather dubious warehouse on the docks at Hull.'

'I see.' Karen sipped her sherry. 'I – I can't help feeling surprised, that's all.'

'Surprised? About what?' He was still standing, some distance away from her it was true, but his presence was vaguely intimidating.

'That – that Daddy should ask you to give me a message.'

'He didn't.' Alexis finished his whisky and poured himself another, flinging himself into an armchair near the door, draping his leg lazily over one arm. 'I offered to let your mother know.'

Karen turned, staring at him over the rim of her glass. 'Then – then why—'

'Why come to the school for you? Guess!' His tone was sardonic.

Karen placed her unfinished drink on the leather surface of the desk. 'I wouldn't presume to do so,' she replied, in a stiff little voice.

'No. Because you know why.' Alexis swallowed more of his whisky. 'Or do you want me to spell it out for you? I wanted to see you.'

Karen rose rather agitatedly to her feet. 'I don't think there's any point in continuing this conversation.'

'Why not?' He had not risen, but his eyes were very intent.

'Because – well, because it's too – too personal. You brought me here without my permission, for a drink, or so you said. Well, I've had a drink, and now I'd like to go home.'

Alexis's expression grew brooding. 'Sit down!' he

muttered grimly. 'And stop behaving as if I was about to rape you! If I decide to do that, I shan't choose the study of my own home!'

Karen caught her breath. 'Will you ask Blake to get my coat?'

'Why are you afraid of me?'

'I'm not afraid of you.' Karen twisted her fingers together painfully.

'Then why are you running away?'

'This is ridiculous . . .'

'I agree.'

He finished his whisky and dropped the glass carelessly on to the carpet. Karen looked at it in amazement, her first instincts to go and pick it up again. It was such an exquisite piece of crystal, and he had discarded it without a second thought. Surely that ought to tell her something, she thought desperately. With a helpless shrug of her slim shoulders she moved towards the door. Blake would give her her coat, and she could easily walk home. It wasn't all that far.

But as she passed Alexis he moved with deceptive swiftness and reaching out, caught her wrist, pulling her down on top of him in the comfortable chair. Karen was taken by surprise, but she struggled furiously, pressing her hands against his chest, trying to get away from him. She could feel the hard muscles of his thighs beneath hers, and smell the warmth of his body. He was half smiling, restraining her effortlessly, and she felt a hopeless sense of inevitability.

'Let me go!' she demanded tremulously. 'I'm not one of your women! You should have invited Shirley for a drink! She would have appreciated this!'

'And don't you?' he inquired lazily, his fingers round the soft flesh of her upper arms, holding her a couple of inches away from him.

'No. No, I – I hate you!'

'You don't hate me, Karen,' he murmured, his thumbs

moving rhythmically against the thin material of the white blouse she was wearing. 'You hate yourself because I can make you feel this way.'

'What way?' she choked indignantly.

'Oh, Karen, you know – what way—'

He jerked her towards him then, imprisoning her hands against his chest, his mouth fastening on to hers with compulsion. She clenched her teeth desperately, pressing her lips together, but it was useless. Alexis was standing for no resistance this time. One hand moved across her shoulder to her neck, unbuttoning her blouse and sliding inside to grip her throat caressingly. His fingers were hard and cool against her flesh and Karen felt an awful weakness overwhelming her as she sank lower in the chair beneath his weight. When he released her mouth and lowered his head to kiss her throat she caught the skin at the side of his neck between her teeth and bit as hard as she could.

Blood spurted into her mouth and his yell of pain erupted as she let him go. The diversion gave her a moment to struggle free of him and she sped across the room to stand panting against the farthest wall. Alexis was levering himself up in the chair, a hand pressed to his neck through the fingers of which she could see blood oozing stickily. A sense of remorse gripped her as she watched him, and with trembling lips, she said: 'You'd better go to the bathroom. It seems to be bleeding quite a lot.'

Alexis's face was grim. 'You little—' He bit off an epithet, bringing down his hand and regarding the blood impatiently.

Karen put a hand to her throat, a sickly feeling invading her stomach. Now that she could see what she had done, she felt worse than ever. The punctures she had made showed up red against the unnaturally pale area around, and blood was running freely down to his collar.

'Do you want me to – to bathe it for you?' she asked uneasily.

85

Alexis rose to his feet, but although she stepped backward in alarm, he did not approach her. He went instead to the desk, lifting a silver cigar case out of a drawer and opening it used the shiny interior as a kind of mirror.

'My God!' he muttered furiously. 'What the hell did you do that for?'

Karen drew a trembling breath. 'May I go home now?'

'Yes – go!' He looked at her with dislike. 'Blake will take you. I'll speak to him.'

'That's not necessary. I can walk.'

'I said Blake will take you.' His tone brooked no refusal and she watched helplessly as he found some tissues to salve the bleeding and then opened the door to the hall. 'Blake!'

The manservant came at once, the smile on his face disappearing as he saw the blood on his employer's neck. 'Y – yes, sir?'

Alexis moved irritably. 'I want you to take Miss Sinclair home. Will you do that?'

'Are you all right, sir?' Blake was concerned.

'Yes, of course I'm all right.' Alexis was impatient. 'I've cut myself, that's all.'

'Yes, sir.' Blake looked beyond Alexis to where Karen was still standing. 'I'll get your coat, miss.'

'Thank you.'

Karen moved forward slowly, but Alexis walked into the hall ahead of her, crossing to the stairs to mount them two at a time. He disappeared along the landing and she was left there alone to wait for Blake.

The manservant returned a few minutes later having put on a jacket and helped her into her coat. Then he glanced rather doubtfully up the stairs. 'Are you ready to leave, miss?'

Karen looked upstairs too and then she made a helpless movement of her shoulders. 'Yes. Yes, I'm ready.'

She had the distinct feeling that if he said much more

she would burst into tears there and then, but to her relief he seemed to accept what she had said and opened the outer door.

In no time at all, it seemed, the big Aston Martin was slowing to a halt outside her home, and gathering together the exercise books from the back seat, she managed to thank Blake politely.

The manservant was courteous, but she could tell he was more concerned with Alexis than with her, and was obviously eager to get back to the house and assure himself that he was all right.

Karen's feelings were less easy to assimilate. She felt she didn't know herself any more. Alexis had deserved what she had done. He had deliberately destroyed the futile defences she had raised against him, and she had been right to use the only weapon left to her.

So why was it that instead of feeling relieved and triumphant, she had this terrible feeling of remorse inside her? Why regret something which had saved her from humiliation and the destruction of self-respect?

She walked up the path to the door in a state of deep depression, despising the weakness inside her that urged her to go back to the house in Moorcourt and beg Alexis to forgive her for what she had done . . .

CHAPTER SIX

ABOUT a week later, Karen's father came home from work one evening looking particularly pleased with himself. He entered the living-room humming, and went straight to the fire to warm his hands. Then he smiled cheerfully at his wife and daughter who were having a cup of tea together before preparing the evening meal.

Laura looked up at him tolerantly. 'I know it's thawing, and there are crocuses out in the front garden, but I didn't realize that spring was actually here.'

Her husband straightened and turned to warm his back. 'Very amusing,' he remarked amiably. 'I gather you are referring to me.'

'To your demeanour, yes.' Laura rose to her feet. 'Do you want a cup of tea?'

'That would be nice.' Her husband touched her cheek. 'You're looking rather attractive this evening.'

Laura sighed. 'What is it? Have you won something? Or has Alexis Whitney given up his managership?'

Karen went cold inside. Since the night Alexis had taken her to his house for a drink she had heard nothing about him. Her mother had accepted her explanation that he had called at the school to tell her about her father working late rather than make a special journey to the house without question, and she had tried to put all thoughts of him out of her mind.

'As a matter of fact,' her father was saying, swinging backwards and forwards on to his heels and toes, 'it is to do with Whitney. He's not at work.'

'Why?' Karen couldn't prevent the question, and her mother turned to look at her impatiently. However, her father had no such reservations.

'He's ill. Been in bed a couple of days, I believe. He

wasn't in yesterday, but I thought nothing of that. He's often away for days visiting warehouses, that sort of thing. But Summerton came to my office this morning and explained that he wasn't well.'

'Do you know what's wrong with him?' Karen refused to meet her mother's questioning gaze.

Her father shook his head. 'I don't know. Cold, I expect. What else could it be?' He snorted cheerfully. 'Unless he's got blood poisoning.' He laughed.

Now it was Laura's turn to be curious. 'Why should he have blood poisoning?'

'Well, he had this – kind of injury to his neck. He had a plaster over it, but I went into his office one day when he had taken it off, and if you ask me someone's bitten him. Oh, he said it was a cut, but it didn't look like a cut to me.'

Laura clicked her tongue exasperatedly. 'I'm sure you're exaggerating, Dan.'

'No, I'm not.' Karen's father chuckled. 'Some kind of she-cat did it, if you ask me, and I don't mean the four-legged variety.'

To Karen's relief, her mother merely made a disparaging movement of her shoulders, and walked out into the kitchen to start preparing dinner. It was as well she had not examined her daughter's face too closely or she might have seen what Karen was trying desperately to hide.

All the same, Karen could not dismiss what her father had said from her mind. Was it possible she was responsible for Alexis's illness, and if so, what ought she to do about it? What could she do about it?

She lived with the problem for two days, during which time she waited anxiously for her father to make some further explanation. But none was forthcoming and as Alexis was still off work, she realized she would have to go to Alexis's house and find out for herself. Blake would be there to mediate, and what was more natural but that she should make an inquiry on her father's behalf?

She walked up to Moorcourt after work on Friday evening. Ray as usual was having his choir practice, so she did not have to tell any lies to him, and her mother expected her home a little later than usual, after she had done some shopping.

Apart from the fact that a newspaper was jutting through the letter-box the place looked deserted, and Karen felt a twinge of apprehension. Perhaps Alexis had gone away, down to his father's home.

She rang the bell twice and waited. There were no sounds coming from inside the house and she frowned. Even if Alexis had gone away, surely Blake would still be here.

But no one came to answer the door and on impulse she walked round the back of the building. She was glad of the high concealing wall surrounding the place. She had no desire to be observed prowling about Alexis's garden by someone like Lucy Summerton, for example.

She looked through a window into a large kitchen with modern, streamlined fittings, but there was no sign of anyone. Only a breadboard rested untidily on the table and beside it a half-eaten loaf of bread, which struck her as being rather odd.

She frowned. Perhaps Alexis was asleep and Blake had gone to the shops. She hesitated. She would knock once more and if no one answered the door she would have to go.

Picking up a stone, she hammered on the back door, hearing the sound echoing hollowly round the house. It was twilight after a rather dismal day, and there was something rather eerie about standing there in the shadow of a clump of stark elms trying to summon life from an obviously dead building.

She was about to turn away when she heard sounds behind the heavy door, and after a few moments it swung a few inches inward and a tall figure, half concealed by the fading light, appeared. As her eyes accustomed themselves to the gloom she saw to her amazement that it was Alexis who stood there, swaying slightly, his face pale and drawn, the growth of several days' beard on his chin.

'Karen?' he muttered nasally, almost as though he couldn't believe his eyes. 'What do you want?'

Karen made an awkward gesture and then realized that he was only wearing a knee-length dressing robe and that his feet were bare on the parquet flooring. Although it was much milder than of late, it was still very cold, and she could see he was shivering.

'May I come in?' she asked quickly, and with a helpless shrug he stood aside and allowed her to enter.

They faced one another in the gloomy kitchen, but Karen was more concerned about him now than about her reasons for coming here. 'Please,' she said. 'Let's go through on to the carpeted floor. You'll catch your death out here.'

Alexis put a weary hand round the back of his neck. 'I'm all right,' he muttered, but he sounded terrible. It was obvious he had 'flu, and that it had invaded his chest as well.

'Please,' she begged again, and with a defeated gesture he led the way through to the wide hall. Once there, he leant against the banister and said:

'What do you want?'

Karen ignored him. 'Where's Blake?'

'Blake?' He seemed confused, as though the effort of thinking was too much for him.

'Yes, Blake! Where is he?'

'Oh, he had to go down to London. His mother's been taken ill. He left yesterday afternoon.'

'And you've been alone since then?' Karen was aghast.

'I'm not an invalid!' remarked Alexis dryly, but then began to cough as though to prove himself wrong.

'You ought to be in bed!' she exclaimed anxiously.

'I was. Until you started ringing bells and hammering on the door!'

'Oh, I'm sorry.' Karen felt a stab of compassion. 'Have you had anything to eat or drink today?'

'I'm not hungry.' He raked a hand through his hair, and as he did so she saw the scar she had left on his neck. But it was not inflamed or angry-looking, so obviously that had not poisoned him. 'Look, can you say what you have to say and go? I feel lousy!'

'Why I came isn't important,' stated Karen, unfastening her coat. 'Go back to bed. I'm going to make you some tea.'

'No, you're not.' He was quite definite about that. 'I don't need anything, and besides, Blake will probably be back in the morning.'

Karen ignored him and draped her coat over the banister. 'Please,' she said again, 'let me make you something. I want to.'

Alexis regarded her wearily. 'Why? I thought you hated me.'

Karen flushed. 'Go back to bed. You need the rest.'

'Do I? Why?'

'Because you're ill,' she exclaimed.

'Who cares?' His tone was ironic, but it shredded her resolve to remain indifferent to him.

'I care,' she answered fiercely. 'Now, will you go back to bed?'

Alexis studied her averted face for a few minutes longer and then without a word he turned and went upstairs. Karen watched him until he was out of sight before re-entering the kitchen and switching on the fluorescent light.

She drew the venetian blinds before making a cursory exploration. There was plenty of food in the refrigerator, she found, steaks, chops, vegetables and salad. There was also a meat pie, but she sensed that Alexis would want nothing so heavy in his condition.

She enjoyed preparing the meal. She seldom had much opportunity to use her cooking skills at home as her mother usually did everything herself, but here she had a free hand.

She made some toast, scrambled some eggs with a light flavouring of cheese, and added a small salad. Then she made a pot of tea and after finding a tray and a cloth she set everything upon it.

The hall was shadowy, and she found the light before ascending the stairs. On the first landing there were several doors, and she hesitated a moment before approaching one that stood slightly ajar. She had chosen correctly, and when she propelled the door open with her shoulder she found herself in Alexis's bedroom.

It was a large room, like all the rooms in the house, but it was austerely furnished in plain woods with only the apricot bedspread and curtains to add some colour. There was a large, old-fashioned fourposter bed, and it was in this that Alexis was lying. He had shed his dressing gown before getting into bed, and the tanned contours of his shoulders were visible as he lay, half on his stomach, one hand pushed up under his pillows as though to support his head. He appeared to be asleep and Karen stood looking at him doubtfully for a few minutes. There was something infinitely vulnerable about anyone in sleep and she was aware of a disturbing sensation in the pit of her stomach.

'Alex!' she said his name softly, but there was no reaction and with a sigh she looked down at the loaded tray. Obviously, for the moment he wanted nothing.

Turning, she left the room again and went back downstairs. In the kitchen she regarded the scrambled eggs thoughtfully, and then on impulse she seated herself at the kitchen table and tackled them with surprising enjoyment. She could easily make some more later, and there was no point in wasting them.

When the washing up was done she glanced at her

watch. It was almost six. Her mother would be beginning to get concerned about her, but what could she do? She didn't intend leaving here until she was sure that Alexis was fit to be left alone.

On impulse, she went through to his study, and closing the door picked up the telephone and dialled her parents' home. Her mother answered, sounding relieved to hear Karen's voice.

'Where are you?' she exclaimed. 'Dinner's almost ready!'

'Well, actually, I called at Melanie's,' said Karen, crossing her fingers guiltily. 'And I'm still here. She's not well, she's full of cold, and I've promised to stay and keep her company this evening.'

Laura sounded put out. 'But what about your dinner?'

'I can easily have something here. A snack will do. You don't really mind, do you, Mum?'

Laura sighed. 'I suppose not. Although you could have rung me sooner.'

'I didn't decide to stay until a few minutes ago. Sorry.'

'Oh, very well,' Laura gave her approval. 'What time will you be home?'

'I'll ring you if I expect to be late,' said Karen quickly.

'What about Ray?'

'You know I don't usually see Ray on Friday evenings. But if he does come round, you can explain, can't you?'

'All right. See you later, then.'

Returning to the kitchen, Karen wandered round aimlessly for a while, looking into all the cupboards and familiarizing herself with their contents. Then, tiring of this, she went back into the hall and by a process of elimination opened all the doors until she found a room that looked like the lounge. There was an enormous television there, but she didn't feel like watching that just now, so she examined the contents of the bookcase instead. Obviously, most of the furniture in the house had been there for years, since Jeff Pierce's time, but as he had been a widower and had only rented the house from the company, after his retirement he had gone to live with his married daughter and very little had been changed.

She found a rather dated thriller and settled down to read for a while, but although she read the words they meant little to her. She was totally involved with what was going on upstairs.

The small French clock was chiming eight when she heard Alexis coughing, and leaving the lounge she made her way back upstairs. It was dark now and without putting on a light she couldn't see whether he was asleep or not, so she stood for a few seconds listening to his breathing, trying to decide whether he was awake. When a small bedside lamp was unexpectedly illuminated she almost jumped out of her skin. Alexis had leant across to put it on and was now propped on one elbow regarding her with eyes that were narrowed against the sudden brightness. There was a mat of hair on his chest, she saw, several shades darker than his hair, and his skin looked brown and smooth. She had the almost irresistible desire to touch him, but his first words brought her to her senses. Blinking, he said: 'What the hell are you doing here?'

Karen shrugged nervously. 'I heard you coughing and I came to see if you were awake.'

'You heard me coughing!' He obviously found this incomprehensible. 'How could you do that?'

'I was downstairs.' Karen caught her lower lip between her teeth. 'I came up earlier with some food, but you were sleeping.'

Alexis ran a perplexed hand down his chest. 'You were downstairs? How did you get in?'

'You let me in.' Karen sighed. 'Don't you remember?'

Alexis sank back against his pillows as though the effort to support himself was too much for him. 'I guess so,' he muttered, but she realized he did not. From the stertorous sound of his breathing and the beads of sweat filming his forehead she knew he had quite a fever and a doctor was what was needed here.

'Look,' she said carefully. 'You've got 'flu, and it's quite obvious that you can't cope here alone. Let me call your doctor—'

'No! I don't need a doctor.' He was adamant.

'But you do,' she protested. ' 'Flu is a serious illness!'

'Then what are you doing hanging about here? Aren't you afraid I'll contaminate you—' He broke off to cough harshly and Karen looked away.

'Alexis, please,' she exclaimed. 'Be sensible! Unless you stay in bed, it's going to get worse.'

'I am in bed,' he remarked wearily.

'I know you are now. But from the state of the kitchen you've been going downstairs for drinks and things when you shouldn't move out of this room.'

'And what would you suggest I do? Remain thirsty?'

'No. Let the doctor provide a nurse—'

'No, thank you.' He interrupted her before she could finish.

'You made my father see a doctor.'

'Your father's past middle-age. I'm not. Look, this is getting us nowhere. Why don't you just accept that I'm not seeing a doctor, and that I'll cure myself, given time?' He closed his eyes and then opened them again. 'Why should you care what happens to me?'

Karen bent her head. 'I should care about any human being who seems bent on injuring himself.'

'Would you?' Alexis sighed. 'I wonder.'

Karen hesitated. Then she said: 'Are you hungry now? Do you want anything?'

'I'm thirsty, that's all,' he admitted reluctantly.

'All right, I'll get you something to drink.'

Glad of the activity, Karen left the room and sped back downstairs again and into the kitchen. There were bottles of cordial in one of the cupboards she had opened earlier, and she found a jug, diluted the liquid liberally, and added ice for good measure. Then she put the jug and a glass on a small tray and went back upstairs.

Alexis gulped the fruit cordial greedily, and lay back on his pillows, exhausted by the effort. Karen stood helplessly beside the bed, wishing she had more knowledge of how to treat 'flu. All she had to go on was her father's experiences, but he had had the assistance of antibiotics to make him well.

Alexis looked tired, but a sardonic expression crossed his lean face. 'Well?' he said. 'Are you leaving now?'

Karen smoothed her finger down the seam of her skirt. 'If you want me to.'

He shook his head slowly. 'What's that supposed to mean?'

'Is there no one I can inform about your illness? Your father, perhaps—'

'No!'

He was more adamant than before, and Karen looked down at him despairingly. How could she go and leave him to fend for himself in this state? She was all too aware of the dangers involved in not taking 'flu seriously. She didn't try to analyse her reactions then. She didn't stop to consider that this man was merely her father's superior, that their relationship so far had been compounded of arguments and confrontations with Alexis showing little or no concern for her feelings, that anyone else would simply walk out of the house and consider his behaviour wholly foolhardy, but nevertheless his own affair.

Karen couldn't do that. Her mind was made up as she walked towards the bedroom door. 'Is there anything else I can get you?'

Alexis moved his head from side to side. 'No.'

Karen nodded. 'Very well, then. Good night.'

'You're leaving?' Was that faint regret in his voice?

Karen paused by the door. 'What else?' she asked, and going out she drew the door to behind her.

Downstairs again she entered the study and picked up the telephone. Her mother answered as before and in rather uneven tones Karen explained that she had decided to stay the night with Melanie. Her mother put up less opposition than she had expected, but as she could hear the buzz of voices in the background she guessed her parents had company that evening and Laura didn't want to spend too long talking to her daughter on the telephone.

That done, Karen returned to the lounge and stood looking about her with thoughtful eyes. At present the house was comfortably warm from the heating of the radiators, but if this system was comparable to others she had seen no doubt later on it would switch itself off for the night. At present she could sleep on the couch, but later it would prove chilly to do so.

Deciding to wait until she was sure that Alexis was asleep before attempting to get herself a blanket from upstairs, she turned out all the lights but a standard lamp beside her chair and settled down with the thriller again.

Despite her tension, she must have dozed, because when she opened her eyes it was much cooler in the room. She looked hastily at the clock and saw it was after midnight. She was amazed. It seemed only minutes ago that she had settled down. She got stiffly out of the chair and stretched, but even as she did so, a sound caused her to drop her arms to her sides almost defensively. Was this what had awakened her, she thought uneasily, and what could it be? It came again, a sort of knocking sound, and on stealthy feet she crept to the door of the lounge and peered out into the hall.

There was nothing to be seen, the hall was in darkness, and the hairs on the back of her neck prickled. But then she saw a thin thread of light beneath the kitchen door and expelled a sigh. Surely no intruder would turn on the lights; it must be Alexis. But what was he doing?

She hesitated. Ought she to go and expose herself to him? So far as he was aware she had left hours ago. What might he say when he found she had not left at all? Her only alternative was to remain where she was, but that would mean waiting another hour before she dared venture out for a blanket and it was getting colder all the time.

Summoning up her courage, she walked swiftly across the hall and reaching out a hand turned the handle of the kitchen door. It gave inwards instantly and for a moment the bright light dazzled her. But then, as her eyes accustomed themselves to the brilliance, she uttered a gasp and stared in amazement at a young woman, dressed in a long, tapestry-designed housecoat, who was trying to knock ice out of a container. The derivation of the noise Karen had heard was obvious, but the identity of the woman was not, and she felt a chilled feeling invading her stomach.

However, if this unexpected confrontation had shocked her, it had equally stunned the other woman. With a startled cry she dropped the ice container on to the floor and gasped: 'Who the hell are you?'

Karen gripped the door handle more tightly. 'I – I might ask you the same question.'

The woman gathered the folds of her housecoat closer about her. 'Let it be sufficient to say that my identity is not in question,' she snapped. 'Who are you? What are you doing here?'

Karen took a deep breath. 'My name is Karen Sinclair, and – and I'm staying here.'

'Like hell you are!' The woman's face was furious. In normal circumstances, Karen could see that she was quite startlingly attractive, but right now, with her claws showing, she was rather hard and coarse.

'I can assure you I am,' Karen went on, controlling her voice with an effort. 'I repeat – who are you?'

99

'What in God's name is going on here?'

A hand descended on Karen's shoulder from behind and she swung round guiltily to find Alexis right behind her, pale and drawn, the bathrobe tightly corded about his waist.

'Alexis,' she began, but she saw his eyes had moved beyond her to the woman standing in the middle of the kitchen. His eyes narrowed ominously and the hand gripping her shoulder tightened until it was an actual agony of pain shooting up into her neck. He stared at the woman for several seconds and then looked down at Karen again, but his expression was inscrutable.

'Well, well,' he said, his voice thickened by congestion. 'It seems we have a visitor, darling.' His inflection was deliberate and to Karen's relief his hand on her shoulder relaxed. But her relief was short-lived, however, as his hand moved up her neck to cause an even more disturbing sensation by caressing the soft skin behind her ear with his thumb. 'You haven't met my stepmother, have you, Karen?'

CHAPTER SEVEN

His stepmother!

Karen was horrified. This then was Michelle Whitney. The woman Lucy Summerton had told her had married Alexis's father because Alexis would not marry her.

Michelle was glaring at them now. 'What's going on?' she demanded. 'I thought you were ill, Alex! Why is she here?'

Alexis used his free hand to draw Karen back against him and she let him. Right now she was too bemused to protest; she had the distinct impression that she was dreaming all this, that soon she might wake up and find herself in her bed, at home. But the feeling of Alexis's hard body beneath the bathrobe seemed real enough, and a yielding sense of lethargy was robbing her of the desire to offer any resistance just at that moment.

'Where else would Karen be?' Alexis was asking softly, but with an underlying note of menace. 'Someone had to look after me, and who better than Karen?' His voice hardened. 'One might ask what you are doing here?'

'But who is she?' There was an edge of hysteria to Michelle's voice now.

Alexis smiled cruelly. 'Didn't she tell you? Why, Karen is my fiancée, of course.'

Now it was Karen's turn to feel bewildered, and faintly resentful, but when she would have struggled away from him his hold on her tightened warningly, and although she felt sure she would regret it later she did not contradict him.

But Michelle did, her rage vituperative. '*Your fiancée!*' she almost screamed. 'I don't believe you! I don't believe you, Alex! You wouldn't – you *couldn't* consider marrying someone like – like her!'

'Be careful, Michelle.' Alexis's voice was chilling. 'Don't say anything you may later regret.'

'Are you threatening me, Alex?'

'Do I need to do that?'

Michelle clenched her fists, venting her spleen in a few moments of uncontrolled verbal hostility which sickened Karen so that she longed to escape. But Alexis would not let her go, and from the tautness of his body she guessed he was using her as a shield against what he might have been tempted to do to his stepmother.

When Michelle finally broke into sobs of recrimination, he said coldly and succinctly: 'Now I'll tell you something, Michelle. You have exactly fifteen minutes to get dressed and get out of here!'

She raised her face to his, but found no compassion there. 'Alex, Alex, I'm sorry . . .' she began, but he pushed Karen away from him and turned away.

'Fifteen minutes, Michelle.'

'But where can I go at this time of night?'

'There are hotels—'

'But in Wakeley, I'd be recognized—'

'That's your problem.'

'Alex, don't make me do this!'

'I'm afraid I must.'

'But why? Alex, why?' Michelle's gaze flickered over Karen, and Karen sensed the malevolence which still lurked in that fleeting glance. 'If – if you're going to marry this – this girl, why can't I stay here too?'

'It wouldn't be – respectable,' replied Alexis, supporting himself against the door jamb. 'Respectability is important in a place like Wakeley.'

'You've never cared about respectability before—'

'Well, perhaps I do now.' Alexis was grim and Karen wondered uneasily how Michelle could stand to be treated so contemptuously in front of another woman. Had she no pride, no self-respect?

As though reading Karen's thoughts, as though realizing that someone else was witnessing her degradation, Michelle seemed to come to a decision. Picking up her skirts, she swept forward, past both of them, and up the stairs without another word. Only then did Alexis's head drop forward on to his chest and Karen realized what a terrific strain this had placed upon him.

'Get me a drink,' he muttered, and Karen went forward to comply, but his arm halted her. 'Not fruit juice,' he added heavily. 'Barley water!'

'Barley water?' she echoed. 'Do you have some?'

'Distilled barley water,' he remarked heavily, straightening. 'Whisky!'

'Oh! Oh, I see.' Karen was still bemused by the events of the past few minutes, but she hurried quickly across the hall and into his study, switching on the lights as she went. When she turned from the drinks cabinet, he was leaning against the door.

'H – here you are,' she stammered, and put a glass into his hand.

'Thanks!' He swallowed half its contents at a gulp and then studied the remainder. Karen stood in the centre of the floor, uncertain of what to do or say next.

But in fact she didn't have to say anything, at least not then. Footsteps sounded on the stairs, and presently Michelle appeared behind Alexis. She was wearing a sable coat now which even Karen could see was worth thousands of pounds, and she was carrying a small suitcase.

'I'm leaving,' she said, looking at her stepson. 'The car's outside. I shall drive into Leeds and stay there.'

Alexis did not say anything, he merely inclined his head in a sardonic gesture, and with a muffled exclamation she walked across the hall and let herself out of the front door, slamming it noisily behind her.

After she had gone, Alexis walked across the hall himself and added a bolt to the already secure fastening of a Yale lock. Then he turned to find Karen hovering nervously in the doorway to the study.

'I suppose I should thank you,' he said, with resignation. 'If you hadn't been here things might have proved – difficult.'

Karen tried to gather her own scattered thoughts. 'Why on earth did you tell her we were engaged?' she exclaimed. It was the first thing that came into her head.

'What would you have had me say? That we were spending the night together?'

Karen shook her head. 'I don't know. What will she think when she finds out it's not true? What if she tells someone?'

'Would you rather have had her tell everyone that you were merely sleeping here? Or do you think she'd have believed me if I'd told her you were my nurse? I can assure you, she wouldn't.'

Karen felt cold sanity creeping back into her bones. 'You're surely not telling me that you said it to protect my reputation!'

Alexis's eyes hardened. 'You wouldn't believe that, of course.'

Karen bent her head. 'I don't know what to believe. Why did she come here?'

'Don't you know?'

'I – I can guess.' Karen felt slightly sick. 'Do you – I mean – is she your mistress?'

'Why do you want to know that?' His voice was harsh.

Karen moved her shoulders helplessly. 'I don't know. I shouldn't have asked. I'm sorry.' She glanced round. 'I – I should go—'

'Don't be silly!' He raked a hand through his hair. 'You can't go now, and you know it! I don't even know why you stayed.' His eyes softened a little as they rested on her flushed cheeks. 'But if it's any interest to you, no – Michelle is not my mistress!'

Karen stared at him. 'But why did she come here?'

Alexis sighed. 'She would like to have something to hold over me where my father is concerned. She would have liked to have confronted me in the morning with the knowledge that she had spent the night in this house, alone with me. She would have liked to have threatened to tell my father what had happened, because knowing him as I do, he would never believe that I wouldn't touch her, given the opportunity.'

'Oh! How – how awful!'

'Yes, isn't it? However, let me assure you that while I may have found Michelle attractive at one time – before she married my father, I might add – right now I find her totally repulsive!'

Karen swallowed hard. 'I see.' Then she seemed to realize that this was the middle of the night and Alexis, no matter how confidently he had faced Michelle, was a sick man. He ought not to be talking at all, let alone standing half naked in the hall of his house. 'I think you ought to go back to bed,' she said quietly. 'If you can tell me where I can find some blankets, I'll sleep on the couch in the lounge.'

Alexis regarded her for a long moment, and then he shook his head. 'Oh, Karen,' he said, and there was a trace of humour in his voice, 'I don't know what to do with you!'

'What do you mean?'

He shook his head. 'It doesn't matter. And as for getting blankets, I absolutely refuse for any nurse of mine to sleep anywhere else than in a bed. There are several perfectly good beds upstairs, and knowing Blake I'm quite sure at least two of them are aired in case of emergencies. And as I'm equally sure you wouldn't agree to share mine, I suggest you use one of them, right?'

Karen's face burned. 'Very well.'

Alexis nodded. 'Good. Shall we go?'

Karen awoke the following morning in a wide bed, soft and luxurious, with silk sheets that caressed her back and thighs. For a moment she couldn't remember where she was, but then remembrance came flooding back and with it the memory of the horrible scene with Michelle Whitney the night before.

She focused on her watch and found it was only a little after eight o'clock. Still, it was time she was up, and almost regretfully she slid out of bed, finding the room comfortably warm as her room at home was never warm. Adjoining the bedroom was an exquisitely furnished bathroom and she took a shower before dressing.

As she brushed her hair with a brush she found on the dressing table she surveyed the room critically. Like the rest of the house the furniture was very old and sprawling, but certainly the bed was as comfortable as any bed she had ever occupied.

Satisfied with her appearance, she left the room and walked along the wide landing. Alexis's door was closed, but after a light tap she opened it and peered inside. His curtains were drawn, but in the gloom she could make out his still form beneath the covers. Closing the door again, she went downstairs and into the kitchen.

The electric kettle didn't take long to boil and while she waited she scanned the headlines of the morning paper she had found pushed through the letter box. There were some letters, too, but they were all official-looking envelopes and she didn't pay a great deal of attention to them.

When the kettle had boiled she made some toast and preparing a tray carried it upstairs. She entered Alexis's bedroom, but he was still asleep and she sighed impatiently. What should she do? Leave it as she had the night before, or wake him up?

However, as she was pondering this he stirred as though becoming aware of someone's presence, and rolled on to his back, taking the sheets with him so that they wrapped about him sarong-wise. He stared at Karen for a while, and then blinked.

'Good morning,' she said, putting down the tray to draw the curtains and allow the faintly glimmering sun to brighten the room. 'How are you feeling?'

Alexis lay still for a few minutes longer and then struggled up on the pillows. 'What time is it?'

'Almost nine.' Karen lifted the tray and carried it to the bedside table. 'I've made you some tea and toast.'

'I don't like tea.' Alexis was uncommunicative.

Karen shrugged. 'It's better for you than coffee when you're not well.'

Alexis grimaced. 'Is it?'

'Yes. Are you going to have it?'

'In a minute.' Alexis sounded moody. 'Did you sleep well?'

'Yes. Did you?'

'No.' He ran a hand over his thickening growth of beard. 'God, I feel a mess!'

'You need a shave, that's all,' replied Karen uncomfortably.

'Do I?' The tawny eyes were penetrating. 'Why did you stay with me, Karen?'

The question was so unexpected that she took a backward step away from the bed before replying. 'I – I was concerned about you.'

'Were you?' He sat up and leaning forward caught her fingers before she realized what he was about to do. Playing with them, he said: 'Aren't you afraid I may decide to tell friend Nichols?'

Karen shook her head firmly. 'You wouldn't do that.'

'Why not?'

'Why should you?'

Alexis shrugged, lying back on his pillows but retaining his hold on her hand so that she had to move nearer the bed. 'Perhaps I meant what I said last night. Perhaps I do want to marry you.'

Karen flushed. 'Don't say things like that.'

'Why not?'

'Because you don't mean them, and besides – I don't want to marry you.'

Alexis's eyes narrowed. 'No?'

'No.'

'Why not?'

'Lots of reasons.'

'Most particularly?'

'I – I don't love you.'

'Is that so important?' His tone was harsh.

'Of course it is,' she retorted indignantly.

'Why? I can give you anything you've ever dreamed about materially—'

'I'm not interested in marriage for those reasons!'

'No?'

'No.' Karen made an involuntary gesture. 'Of course, you can't understand that, can you? The society you move in bases success and happiness on that maxim, doesn't it?'

Alexis's eyes narrowed. 'What do you know about the society I move in?' he asked disparagingly, resisting her attempts to pull her hand free.

'You've only to read the newspapers,' she replied shortly.

'And you believe what you read in the newspapers?'

'Some things – yes.'

'About me?'

'Look, this is silly. Please – drink your tea before it gets cold.'

Alexis ignored her, and with slow deliberate movements raised her hand to his lips, kissing each of her fingers in turn. Karen felt an awful sense of weakness in her lower limbs, but she determinedly forced mundane things into her mind.

'If you'll let go of my hand I'll go and get you some

water for washing and shaving—'

'I am perfectly capable of visiting the bathroom myself, thank you,' he returned ironically, sliding his fingers over her wrist and up her arm, systematically drawing her nearer the bed. 'Come here.'

'No! Alexis—' But her protest was lost in a gasp of dismay as he pulled her down beside him, and rolled over so that the whole weight of his body was imprisoning hers. With one hand he deftly secured both of hers above her head and then looked mockingly down into her face.

'Well?' he challenged huskily. 'What are you going to do now?'

Karen moved her head restlessly from side to side. 'Let me go,' she demanded helplessly. 'Don't you have any shame? I came here to – to see if you were all right. I stayed to look after you. And this is how you repay me—'

'You shouldn't expect any decency from someone like me,' he taunted her, putting his mouth to the curve where her shoulder met her neck. 'Isn't this exactly how you expect me to behave?'

'Yes! Yes, it is!' She gulped. 'And – and you talked about marriage! I – I wouldn't marry anyone like you even if you offered me the Crown Jewels! You don't care about anyone except yourself. I – I hate you!'

His free hand closed round her throat, gripping it with painful insistence as he said: 'Why should I marry a woman who's quite prepared to go to bed with me without that legalizing scrap of paper?'

'There are – other things in marriage!' she gasped.

'Are there? And are you going to tell me also that sex is a very small part of that arrangement!'

'Well – well, it is.'

His lips twisted. 'Really? Well, let me tell you something, unless that – and you know what I mean by *that* – is right, everything else is wrong! You tell me differently, and you're not talking about marriage. You're talking about two individuals living in the same house – legally.'

'For someone who despises it, you seem to know an awful lot about it,' Karen exclaimed, breathing hard.

He shook his head. 'I don't despise it. Just its applications in certain circumstances. Do you know the definition of the word? It means an intimate association – the provision for procreation and sexual gratification. Would you exclude those principles?'

Karen twisted her body with difficulty. 'And you think that excuses your behaviour, is that it?'

'I'm not trying to justify my actions to you, I don't have to.' He bent his head and touched her mouth with his, playing with her lips until she felt her head lifting involuntarily from the pillow to increase that disturbing pressure. But he drew back, and she hated herself for showing him how easily he could arouse her.

'I – I – let me go!' She took a shaking breath. 'My mother will be expecting me back this morning!'

'You'll be back,' he murmured lazily. 'Perhaps a little more experienced than when you left—'

'You – you wouldn't dare!' she choked.

'Wouldn't I?' His expression was derisive. 'Why not?'

'Alexis—' Her voice broke, and suddenly he rolled away from her, turning on to his back, staring grimly up at the ceiling.

For a few moments Karen just lay there, unable to will movement into her lethargic limbs. But finally she came to her senses and scrambled off the bed, smoothing her skirt, fastening the loosened neck of her blouse. She stood for a minute looking down at him, and then she said: 'Do you want some fresh tea?'

He turned cold amber eyes upon her, and she felt herself shrink at that bitter appraisal. 'Just get out of here!' he muttered, and without a backward glance she went.

Although Karen disliked deceiving her parents there was no way she could tell them that she had spent the night in Alexis Whitney's house. Apart from anything else she realized that they were like Alexis's father in that respect; they would never believe she had slept there without sharing his bed.

Instead, she gave them the news they wanted to hear, using Melanie as a substitute, and prayed that they would not discover that six weeks ago Melanie had left Wakeley to go and work in Newcastle.

During the following week her father informed both her and her mother that Alexis was back at work.

'Four days he had off, that was all,' Daniel Sinclair muttered fiercely, 'plus the week-end, of course. He made me have four weeks.'

'Oh, come on, Dan,' exclaimed Karen's mother clicking her tongue. 'It was the doctor who made you stay off, not Alexis Whitney. In any case, I'm relieved to hear he's better. I don't like the thought of anyone being ill.'

'Huh!' Her husband sounded less convinced. 'He's barely through the door again before he's talking about getting these time and motion study chaps from London to come and take a look at this idea of his for doing away with the conveyor.'

'Ah, I see.' Laura chuckled. 'That's what's upsetting you, is it? I thought it wasn't just the fact that he's back at work. How is he feeling anyway?'

Karen's father grunted and took out his pipe. 'The devil looks after his own, I daresay,' he muttered. 'Anyway, things have worked well enough over the years, so why can't he leave well alone now?'

'Oh, Dan!'

Karen's mother sounded impatient and Karen herself, who had been sitting in an armchair by the fire studying some textbooks, rose to her feet and left the room. She couldn't bear to hear her parents discussing Alexis without feeling an awful sense of depression at the knowledge that one way or another she had succeeded in destroying any kind of relationship between them. The past few nights this realization had interfered with her sleep and while she could tell herself that she had been right to behave the way she had, and that Ray was worth a dozen Alexis Whitneys, nevertheless there had been something in their association that by its erasure had left her feeling completely flat.

The weather was improving rapidly, and all traces of snow had disappeared. It was half-term at the comprehensive school that week-end and Karen was eager to accept Ray's suggestion that they spent the week-end in the Lake District. They had done this other years, staying at youth hostels, associating with other young people with similar interests, spending their days walking over the fells. It was exactly what Karen needed; the exertion, the air, the escape from the confines of Wakeley. Certainly, she slept better that week-end than she had done for some time, physically exhausted, and deaf to the stirrings of her conscience.

She returned to school feeling refreshed and grateful to Ray for his gentle, undemanding company.

But her brief period of relaxation was short-lived. On Friday morning there was a telephone call for her during her history period, and Shirley Scott looked at her rather knowingly as she agreed to take charge of the class until Karen's return.

It was Alexis Whitney again, as she had known it would be, and her hand shook as she raised the receiver to her ear.

'Karen? Is that you?'

'Yes. What do you want?' Her voice was stilted. 'I told you – we're not supposed to have private calls during working hours.'

'Would you rather I came to meet you, then? I thought that didn't suit you either. As I recall it, we offended Nichols and created speculation in other quarters.' His tone was dry, but at least he sounded well again, and she despised the feeling of relief that gave her.

'What do you want? I thought – that is – I can't think why you should want to contact me.'

'Can't you?' He paused a moment. 'I need to see you. I have something I want to discuss with you, but not on the telephone. Will you have lunch with me?'

'Today?' She was shocked.

'Yes, today. What time do you have lunch?'

'I – I usually eat in the canteen—'

'I didn't ask where you usually ate. I asked what time.'

'I know that.' Karen was stung by his arrogance. 'In any case, I haven't agreed to have lunch with you.'

'Karen, I need to see you.'

'Why?'

'I'll explain when I see you.'

'Why can't you explain now?'

'Karen!' It was a command.

'Oh, very well. We break from twelve-thirty until two.'

'Fine. I'll pick you up at the gates at – say – twelve-thirty-five, right?'

Karen hesitated. 'All right.'

'Good.' He sounded satisfied and she heard his receiver being replaced.

She replaced her own and sat staring at the phone mutinously. What could he want to speak to her about? Why should he need to do so? She had given up any thought of ever seeing him again, except in passing, so to speak, and now he had destroyed all her newfound release in one fell swoop.

She looked down at what she was wearing critically and felt a ridiculous sense of pleasure that she had chosen to wear her green suède waistcoat and matching skirt that morning. Teamed with a red polo-necked sweater they looked very attractive, the maxi-length skirt only a couple of inches above her ankle.

With an impatient exclamation she got to her feet. What did it matter what she was wearing? After her last encounter with Alexis Whitney she doubted whether his reasons for wanting to see her again had anything to do with her personally. Perhaps it concerned her father.

Shirley regarded her tolerantly when she returned to the history class. 'Your cousin again, I suppose.'

Karen sighed. 'Does it matter?'

'Not to me. But you're taking a chance, you know,' the other girl retorted sharply.

'What do you mean—'

'I mean Ray – that's what I mean!'

Karen flushed. 'I don't see that it's any concern of yours.'

'Isn't it?' Shirley's eyes were challenging. 'There are those among us who find one man more than adequate.'

'You don't understand, Shirley.' Karen gathered her papers together rather impatiently.

'Oh, but I do. If you're playing fast and loose with Ray, then he has every right . . .' Her voice trailed away suddenly and Karen looked up.

'Every right to what?' she asked.

'Oh – nothing.' Now it was Shirley's turn to look embarrassed.

Karen frowned. 'Are you trying to tell me something, Shirley?'

'No. No, of course not.'

Karen wasn't altogether satisfied and would have liked to have questioned her further, but just at that moment the bell rang signifying the end of the period. The pupils began gathering their books together and in the noise and confusion that ensued Shirley slipped away.

As luck would have it, Ray wasn't about when she went to tell him she would not be dining in the canteen after all. It was unfortunate, but she could explain when she returned, she told herself, ignoring the rather guilty feeling which always assailed her when she was associating with Alexis Whitney.

Leaving her coat unfastened, she slung her suède bag over her shoulder and walked briskly up to the school gates. Those pupils who went home for lunch were thronging out of the quadrangle and she was aware of their curious stares as she walked across to where the dark green Aston Martin was parked. Alexis thrust open the door for her from inside and she slid in thankfully, closing the door behind her.

Alexis gave her a brief, comprehensive stare and then set the car in motion. For her part, Karen scarcely glanced at him, but all the same she was conscious of his nearness, and of the intimacy that one look from him could engender.

'I thought we'd eat at the Pipes,' he remarked, naming a hotel just outside of Wakeley which had built up quite a reputation for good food. 'Does that suit you?'

'So long as I'm back before two,' replied Karen equably. Then realizing that something more was expected of her, she went on: 'Are you fully recovered from your illness?' in rather taut tones.

'Fully, thank you. I gather you haven't been smitten with the bug yourself.'

'No. I've been lucky.'

Karen looked through the windows. Their conversations always seemed to be like this – either disturbingly personal, or coldly indifferent, like now.

The Pipes Hotel stood in its own grounds. It had once been a private house, but since then it had been extensively modernized and now possessed an aura of taste and elegance not found in more contemporary buildings.

Alexis was not wearing an overcoat over his dark business suit, but Karen left her coat in the vestibule and spent a couple of minutes in the ladies' room checking her make-up before joining him. By common consent they walked into the attractively furnished lounge bar and seated themselves on tall stools by the bar. Karen accepted a Martini, while Alexis had gin and tonic, and covertly studied the other patrons. They were a mixture of business men and women, with a few socialites thrown in for good measure. It was an expensive establishment and in consequence only attracted the more affluent members of Wakeley society.

Alexis spoke to the bartender, answered the casually called greetings which were addressed to him, or applied himself to his drink. He didn't speak to Karen, and she couldn't for the life of her think of anything to say to him, and by the time he had finished his second gin and tonic she was wishing she had not agreed to come. She was still playing with her first Martini, and wondering what on earth he could possibly want to say to her.

However, it seemed he was now ready for food, for he slid off his stool and said: 'Are you going to finish that, or shall we go into the restaurant?'

Karen took a final sip from her glass before pushing it firmly across the counter and taking this as her assent he helped her down from her stool with a casual hand which he withdrew as soon as they began walking out of the bar.

In the restaurant Karen looked at the menu without really seeing it. The variety of main courses staggered her and she hadn't the faintest idea what to choose.

An obsequious waiter appeared at Alexis's elbow, and leaning across the table, he said: 'Have you decided what you want?'

Karen shook her head. 'I – I can't choose.' She hesitated. 'What are you going to have?'

Alexis consulted the menu. 'Fillet steak and salad, I think.'

'Well, I'll have that, too,' she murmured hastily.

'Are you sure?'

'Yes.' She sighed. 'I'm sorry.'

His expression darkened impatiently, but then he gave the order to the waiter, adding that they would have soup to begin with.

The meal was delicious. Even Karen could not fault it, and she found that her appetite was stimulated by the wine Alexis had ordered. But apart from commenting upon the wine and the food, he still said nothing, and she was growing more and more apprehensive, half prepared to believe that whatever he had wanted to say, he had changed his mind about it.

She refused a liqueur with her coffee, and glanced surreptitiously at her watch. It was a little after one-thirty and it was ten minutes' drive back to the school. Deciding she had to take the plunge, she said: 'Are you going to tell me why you invited me here or not?'

Alexis had been stirring his coffee, staring down into it broodingly; his expression was not encouraging. Now he looked up and the tawny eyes assessed her coldly. 'Of course.'

'Then do you mind getting on with it? It's gone half past one, and I have to leave here soon after a quarter to two if I'm to be back in time.'

He flicked the heavy silvery hair back from his forehead with a careless hand and glanced round the restaurant. 'Very well. It's quite a simple thing really. I want you to do something for me.'

'Me?' exclaimed Karen ungrammatically.

'Yes.' He took the spoon out of his cup and placed it carefully in the saucer. 'I want you to come to London with me next week-end!'

CHAPTER EIGHT

To say Karen was shocked would have been an under-statement. She was amazed, astounded, incredulous!

She stared into those cool amber eyes and for a few moments she could say nothing. Then, shaking her head in a slightly bemused fashion, she broke the silence which had fallen. 'You can't be serious!'

'Why not?' As always he challenged her.

'Well, putting aside the fact that I have no desire to spend a week-end alone with you – why should you need to ask me?'

'Did I say we were to be alone?'

'No, but – but naturally—'

'Yes, naturally, you've fallen into a trap of your own making.' A faint smile twisted his mouth. 'Don't jump to conclusions, Karen. Not until you know all the facts.'

She bent her head, her hair falling in a curtain about her cheeks. 'Whatever the facts are, I'm not interested,' she said, her voice slightly muffled.

'I see.' He lifted his liqueur and tasted it experiment-ally. 'Not even if I tell you that if you don't agree to do as I ask you run the risk of our relationship being made public knowledge?'

'What do you mean?' Her head jerked back.

'Be patient, and I'll explain.' He finished his liqueur and drew out a case of cigars. 'Do you mind?' He indi-cated the cigars.

'Of course not.' Karen clenched her fists uneasily. What was he hatching out now?

Exhaling smoke into the air above their heads, Alexis regarded her calmly. 'My father and his wife celebrate their seventh wedding anniversary next week-end, at Falcons, my father's house near Maidenhead. I've been invited to join the festivities.'

Karen digested this. 'And you want me to accompany you?'

Alexis studied the glowing tip of his cigar. 'Let me put it this way: Michelle will not have told my father about you. How could she? So far as he is concerned, she hasn't seen me since I last visited London. But *she* knows, and it is, shall we say, unfortunate, that these celebrations come so soon after – a certain incident. Were I to arrive at Falcons without my fiancée, I guarantee within a few days your parents would know of our association—'

'But why?' Karen interrupted him. 'Why?'

Alexis sighed. 'Michelle has a malicious streak. She won't have forgotten that you were present – that you were a party to her humiliation. But only you and I know exactly how much mischief she could cause.'

'But you can't mean to tell me that she would actually contact my mother and father—'

'Oh, no. Nothing so simple, or condemning, as that. The information would be given to the local press, to use as they choose. It's a common enough angle. She would be gambling, of course. You might not care that your name is being linked with mine in such circumstances, but I'm pretty sure she's aware of the confined atmosphere of a place like Wakeley and the chances of your appreciating such publicity are slim.'

'But – but why should you care – about me?'

'I don't,' he responded chillingly. 'But I do care about the mill, and I've no wish to antagonize your father into doing something we might both regret.'

'I – I see.' Karen rested her elbows on the table, her palms cupping her face. 'What a mess!'

'Do you want that liqueur now?'

Karen blinked. 'A liqueur?' she echoed absently. 'Oh – oh, no.' She shook her head, and then caught a glimpse of her watch. It was nearly ten minutes to two. 'Gosh, I've got to go. I'm going to be late!'

'Don't panic!' Alexis rose to his feet, summoning the waiter. He signed the cheque, added a tip, and disregarding the waiter's thanks helped Karen up. 'Come along. We can talk later.'

The traffic in the town centre occupied Alexis's attention to the exclusion of everything else, and Karen sat in frozen silence wondering how on earth she was going to find reasons to go away for a week-end at the end of March.

When they reached the school and she was about to get out, Alexis said: 'We've got to get this settled sooner or later.' He frowned. 'I've got a dinner party this evening, and my uncle and his wife are coming for the week-end. It will have to be one day next week. How about Monday?'

Karen drew a shaking breath. 'I – I'll ring you,' she said. 'That's the best arrangement.'

'When – and where?'

'At – at your house. I know the number. Say – Monday evening.'

Alexis's eyes softened. 'Don't look so worried! It's not the end of the world, you know. You might even enjoy it – the week-end, I mean.'

Karen made a helpless little gesture and slid out of the car. How could he joke about it? Not when she was feeling so totally out of her depth.

She watched the car draw smoothly away, and then ran down the drive and into the school. She just had a moment to shed her outdoor things before joining her class for a literature session.

There were no breaks in the afternoon, and as Ray had choir practice immediately after the last period she had no chance to speak to him and explain why she had been out at lunchtime. She half expected he might appear that evening and demand an explanation, but he didn't, and she went to bed feeling utterly miserable.

On Saturday afternoon, they had arranged to go into

Leeds. Karen wanted to get a few things and then they were going to have a meal before going to see a film they had both wanted to see. Karen was changing into her navy blue trouser suit in her bedroom when she heard Ray arrive and her father take him into the living-room where he was watching the sports programmes on television. He and Ray both supported Leeds United football club, and were constantly discussing tactics and why or why not they should have won their last game.

Karen came downstairs almost reluctantly. She was dreading the moment when she would have to invent a reason for being absent the previous afternoon.

Ray greeted her amiably enough, however, and after a few more words with her father they left. It was a glorious spring afternoon, the air warming imperceptibly, and everywhere trees were burgeoning with life. They got into Ray's car, he started the engine, and they drove away.

'I'm sorry I missed you yesterday,' remarked Karen, deciding the best method of defence was attack.

'When? At lunchtime?' Ray was casual.

'Yes. I went out.'

'I know.' Ray glanced her way. 'I saw you.'

Karen felt the hot colour flood up into her cheeks. 'You – saw – me?'

'Yes. And Whitney.' Ray sounded resigned. 'So don't bother to think up some elaborate excuse.'

Karen's fingers tightened round her handbag. 'All right, I won't.' Her voice was tight and only slightly shaky.

Ray clicked his tongue impatiently and looked at her again. 'Well, what do you expect me to say? That I'm pleased you're going out with him behind my back?'

'I – I'm not going out with him behind your back,' she protested indignantly.

'But you weren't going to tell me you'd had lunch with him yesterday, were you?'

Karen sighed. 'No.'

'There you are, then.'

'You don't understand. There were – things – we had to discuss.'

'What – things?'

Karen lifted her shoulders. 'I can't explain.'

'You see!' Ray was accusing.

'Oh, Ray, I'm sorry. I – I'd like to tell you, really I would. But – but you wouldn't understand.'

'Try me!'

'I can't.' Karen looked at him unhappily. 'Oh, I know how it must sound but – well, I can't help it.'

'Are you in love with him?' Ray was abrupt.

'In love? With Alexis Whitney? Of course not.'

'Why of course not? He seems to find you more than attractive.'

'That means absolutely nothing,' Karen exclaimed impatiently. 'Alexis thinks women are easy game. Just because I won't—' She halted abruptly, realizing exactly what she had been about to confess to.

But Ray wouldn't let it rest there. 'Just because you won't what?' he asked curiously. 'Come on! You've got so far, say it all!'

'It's nothing. I meant nothing.'

'Just how well do you know this chap?' asked Ray angrily. 'Apart from seeing him at your house and that night he picked you up from work, how many more times have you been out with him?'

'I haven't – that is – oh, Ray, if you must know, I knew him years ago. Before I left school. When he was at university.'

'I see.' Ray absorbed this with obvious distaste. 'So how well did you know him then?'

Karen shrugged. 'Quite well.'

'What's that supposed to mean?'

'It means – quite well.' Karen played with the strap of her shoulder bag. 'Ray, I haven't been to bed with him, if that's what you're driving at!'

'I should jolly well hope not.' Ray was flushed now as though such topics embarrassed him. Then he frowned. 'But I suppose that's what you were about to say, isn't it? That's why he finds you – different. Because you don't sleep around.'

'I suppose so.' Karen bent her head.

'And is that what all this is about? Does he have some kind of hold over you?' A spurt of inspiration hit him. 'Of course! I bet your father doesn't know you were once his girl-friend, does he?'

Karen hesitated. 'Well – no. No, he doesn't.'

Ray's fists clenched round the wheel. 'And is he threatening to tell your father—'

'Oh, no, no! Nothing like that.' Karen was horrified. The last thing she wanted was for Ray to get involved in all this.

'Then why are you associating with him? Unless you want to do so, of course!'

'I've told you. We had something to discuss.'

'What?' Ray was becoming angry now and she couldn't altogether blame him.

Taking a deep breath, she said: 'Well, if I tell you, will you keep it in confidence?'

Ray frowned. 'Naturally.'

'All right.' Karen sighed again. 'Do you remember a couple of weeks ago, Alexis was ill?'

Ray accelerated to pass a slow-moving car before saying: 'Yes, I remember. Your father was delighted because he was in charge again.'

'That's right. Well, Alexis had 'flu.'

'So?'

'So I went up to his house to see how he was.'

'You did what?' Ray was horrified.

'I went up to the house to see how he was.' She paused for a moment. 'He wasn't at all well. He was obviously running a temperature and Blake – that's his manservant

– was away, visiting his mother down south. Alexis was there alone, and there was no one to look after him.'

'Poor thing!' Ray was sarcastic.

'Yes – well, anyway, I stayed.'

'*You stayed!*' Ray had to drag his eyes back on to the road. 'What do you mean? Overnight?'

'Yes,' and as Ray would have interrupted her again, she went on: 'Please! Give me a chance to explain! Don't go jumping to conclusions!'

'What the hell else am I supposed to do?' Ray was furious now, and Karen was doubtful whether she should go on.

'Anyway,' she said at last, 'I slept – downstairs.' After his attitude she couldn't tell him anything else, even though it was ridiculous to assume that one place was less provocative than another. 'And I was woken about midnight by a noise, and when I went to investigate I found this woman in the kitchen.'

'What woman?'

'If you give me a chance I'll tell you.'

'All right. Go on, then.'

'It was Michelle Whitney, Alexis's stepmother.'

'So?'

Karen sighed. This was proving more and more difficult. 'Well, she saw me there.'

'And?' Ray was obviously finding it hard to control his temper.

'That's what we had to discuss.'

'You mean today?'

'Yes. You see, Alexis tried to protect my reputation by telling his stepmother that – that I was his – his fiancée—'

'My God!' Ray raised his eyes heavenward.

'—and now next week-end it's his father's wedding anniversary. He – he lives near London. And if I don't go along with Alexis, it'll look – that is, they'll think – well, it might all come out. About me staying at the house and

124

so on.'

Ray stood on the brakes, almost throwing her forward through the windscreen, and the small car came to an abrupt halt. 'Do you mean to tell me all this has been concocted to lead up to the fact that next week-end you and Whitney intend to spend a sneaky couple of days together!'

Karen was indignant. 'Of course not. It's the truth.'

Ray gave a sceptical grunt. 'You don't say!'

'But it is.' Karen was desperate. 'Ray, you asked me to tell you the truth, and I have. I don't know what more I can say.'

'You could begin by crediting me with a little more intelligence than you have,' retorted Ray angrily. 'Do you honestly expect me to swallow all that? You spend a night with Whitney, alone in his house, without anything happening between you, and just because his old lady happens to see you there—'

'She's not his old lady,' cried Karen. 'And exactly what are you accusing me of?'

Ray hunched his shoulders, then he half turned away from her, slumped in his seat. 'Oh, I don't know,' he muttered. 'I don't know.'

Karen watched him unhappily for several minutes, and then she said: 'Ray! Ray, please! I'm telling you the truth.'

Ray remained where he was for a little while longer and then he looked back at her. 'If I'd told you that I'd spent a night alone with some female, how would you feel?'

Karen stared down at her folded hands. Her answer was clear. She ought to say that she would not have liked it, that she would feel as suspicious as Ray was feeling. But if she was honest with herself she would admit that if Ray had told her something like that she would have accepted it, simply because Ray was not the type to indulge in any kind of promiscuity. She sometimes wondered if he ever had, or whether he was as inexperienced as she was herself.

But now she nodded and said: 'I take your point. Nevertheless, it happened, and there's nothing I can do about it.'

'No.' Ray was grudgingly aware of this. 'But this weekend,' he went on. 'You can't expect me to condone it.'

'No.' Karen accepted this.

'So,' Ray wound down his window and produced cigarettes, offering one to her which she refused. After lighting his own, he went on: 'You'll have to refuse, I suppose, unless . . .'

'Unless what?' She looked up.

'Unless he's agreeable that I should come with you.'

Karen's lips parted. 'That you should come with us?' she echoed faintly.

'That's right. Why not? You're going for these wedding celebrations, aren't you? Why shouldn't he invite more than one guest?'

Karen couldn't answer him. His suggestion buzzed around in her head like an angry insect. Ray – come to London with them? It was ludicrous!

And yet was it? Wasn't it exactly the sort of suggestion she should jump at? She professed not to want to go with Alexis. She argued that she was only going to protect her parents. If Ray was there as well, there was nothing to worry about. And in addition she had a built-in reason for being away. Her parents would not raise any opposition to her spending another week-end in the Lake District with the man they expected her to marry. And as Ray had said, there were bound to be a lot of guests at this party. One more or less wouldn't make that much difference. But what would Alexis say?

'Well?' Ray had been watching the play of emotions across her face. 'Don't you think he'll agree?'

Karen wet her dry lips. 'I don't know. I'd have to ask him first.'

'And will you?'

'If that's what you want.'

Ray uttered an exclamation. 'It should be what you want, too.'

Karen shrugged. 'I – it is!' She tried to calm her shaking nerves. 'I – I'll ring him on Monday.'

'Good.' Ray threw away his half-smoked cigarette. 'And now I suppose we can go to Leeds.'

'If you like.' Karen managed a faint smile, and Ray started the engine without mentioning it again.

Throughout that day and the day that followed, Karen tried to behave normally, but it was terribly difficult. She couldn't begin to imagine what Alexis's reaction to Ray's suggestion might be, and she wondered what Ray would do if Alexis said no.

Ray, on the surface at least, seemed just as usual. They didn't mention the following week-end, and although from time to time she found him watching her rather closely, in the main nothing appeared to have changed.

Monday dragged by, and when Ray drove her home in the evening, he said: 'When are you going to speak to Whitney?'

Karen frowned. 'I suppose I could do it now, if you like.'

'Fine. There's a kiosk just along here. I'll wait outside.'

She supposed this was a concession. After all, he could have come into the box with her.

But although she allowed it to ring and ring, no one lifted the receiver and she emerged from the kiosk feeling rather apprehensive.

Ray gave her a strange look when she told him. 'Are you sure you rang the right number?'

'Of course I'm sure.' Karen sighed. 'Don't you believe me?'

Ray shrugged. 'I guess so. But it's after five. I'd have thought he'd be home by now.'

'Perhaps he's still at the mill.'

'Why didn't you try there, then?'

'And have Peggy at the exchange recognize my voice? No, thanks.'

'What a tangled web,' quoted Ray mockingly, starting the car again and she hunched her shoulders and wouldn't look at him.

When he left her at her gate, he said: 'I'll come round later. If you've had no success, we can ring then.'

'All right,' Karen nodded, and after allowing him to kiss her swiftly on the mouth she got out of the car.

When her father came home she tried to probe information from him as to whether Alexis had left the mill or not and succeeded in discovering that he had, in fact, been away for the day. This left her wondering what time he was likely to get back, and she had hardly any appetite for the rissoles her mother had prepared for their meal.

But half-way through the meal the telephone rang, and Karen got up to answer it. To her surprise it was Alexis, but before she could express her indignation that he should ring her at home, he said: 'Have you been trying to ring me?'

'Yes,' answered Karen quickly, 'but—'

'I thought it was you,' he interrupted her. 'Blake was out, but he heard the phone ringing as he came in. Before he could answer it, you'd rung off.'

'Who is it, Karen?'

Her mother was standing in the kitchen doorway, and Karen looked up guiltily. 'Oh – er – it's Ray,' she answered unhappily. 'I won't be long.'

Her mother nodded and went back into the kitchen and closed the door. Karen sighed in relief, and Alexis said: 'So I'm to be Nichols, am I?'

'What would you have said if my father had answered the phone?' she challenged him in a low angry tone.

'I'd have thought of something. The current order, for example. Does it matter?'

'I'm not as used to intrigue as you are!'

'What's that supposed to mean?' His tone was cold, and when she didn't answer he went on: 'Well! Have you thought about what I asked you? Are you coming to Falcons with me?'

Karen fingered the receiver uneasily. 'I've thought about it, yes. But it's not that simple.'

'What now?' He sounded bored by it all.

'Ray knows – and – and he wants to come too.'

There was silence for such a long time that she half thought he had rung off, but at last he said: 'I see. You told him, I suppose.'

'I – I had to. He saw us together on Friday lunchtime.

'Indeed. And his coming along – whose suggestion was that?'

'Why – his, of course.' Karen lifted her shoulders. 'Oh, look, Alexis. Ray and I are almost engaged. How would you like it if you were in his position?'

Alexis didn't reply to this. Instead he said: 'And how do you think it will look if the three of us arrive together? Michelle's not stupid, you know.'

'I don't see what else I can say.'

Alexis considered for a moment. 'Maybe – maybe if there was someone else with us – some other girl – she would accept it.'

Karen gasped. 'Another girl?'

'Yes. Someone who could pass for Nichols' girl-friend. You must admit it would look more realistic.'

'As friends of mine, you mean?'

'Yes.'

'But who? I don't know anyone who would do such a thing.'

'Don't you? What about that girl we gave a lift to the other evening – Shirley something or other. She's a friend of Nichols', isn't she? Wouldn't she do it? For a week-end away, all expenses paid.'

Karen stiffened. The idea of taking Shirley Scott into her confidence wasn't appealing. 'And what am I supposed to say to her?'

Alexis hesitated. Then he said: 'Tell her I've invited you and Ray for the week-end. Ask her if she'd like to join the party.'

'But – but she'll think – you're inviting her,' Karen demurred.

'I am.'

'But – but—' Karen couldn't altogether understand her reluctance to agree to such an arrangement.

'But nothing. I know these house parties of my father's. They're not small affairs. There'll be so many people present that by the end of the evening nobody will notice who's with whom.'

'I see.' Karen's voice was almost inaudible.

'Well?' Alexis was impatient now. 'Will you do that?'

'I – I suppose I shall have to. When – when will we leave?'

'On Saturday morning. I could pick you up at home, but I guess you'd rather meet me in the High Street.'

'Yes,' Karen nodded.

'Fine. Well, let's say – about nine-thirty. Subject to alteration by phone, if necessary, right?'

'All right.' Karen's throat felt dry. 'Is that all?'

'I guess so.' Alexis sounded amused. 'What's wrong? Don't you like the arrangements?'

'I don't like any of it!' retorted Karen heatedly. 'Not any of this whole affair.'

CHAPTER NINE

KAREN's first sight of Alexis's father's house was from a cramped position in the rear seat of Alexis's car. The mellowed old building was reassuringly plain and not at all the elaborate kind of background she had expected Alexis to have. Tall spruce trees lining the drive gave glimpses of lawns and terraces overlooking the river, and because it was a warm spring afternoon there were boats on the water making their way upstream, the sound of voices and laughter lingering on the air.

She looked sideways and met Shirley Scott's knowing blue eyes. If only there had been some other way of doing this, she thought for the umpteenth time. It wasn't that there had been any particular difficulties involved in persuading the other girl to come, rather the reverse, but nevertheless Karen couldn't help wishing it was all over and that they were on their way north again.

To her surprise, Ray had been quite enthusiastic about asking Shirley. He had agreed that a foursome was a far more suitable arrangement and as Shirley had been only too willing to accept such an invitation there had been no problem there.

But Karen had had other matters to occupy her. In the end she had confided to her mother that they had been invited to spend the week-end at Alexis's father's home. Mrs. Sinclair had been flabbergasted at first, and then increasingly concerned about Karen's part in all this. Karen's explanation that he had asked Ray first had not quite rung true, particularly as her mother knew of their previous association.

'And does Ray know Alexis Whitney that well?' she had asked suspiciously, and Karen had had to explain that he was only asking them to make up a foursome with

Shirley.

'We were the only people he could ask – mutual friends, so to speak.'

'Well, I shouldn't have thought he'd be interested in Shirley Scott,' retorted her mother. 'I've heard rumours that Lucy Summerton has designs in that direction. And after all, her father has known Howard Whitney since he first went into business.'

Karen turned away. She didn't want to hear about Alexis and Lucy Summerton. 'You never can tell,' she remarked vaguely, but her mother was not put off.

'You just watch your step, Karen,' she said with emphasis. 'I don't altogether care for you going down to London for the week-end, no matter who it's with. Hostelling in the Lake District is one thing, London is quite another.'

'Oh, Mum!' Karen was disparaging. 'Do you honestly believe it makes any difference – surroundings I mean?'

'No – no, I suppose not,' Laura had to agree. 'But just remember, Alexis Whitney is not to be trusted.'

Karen made some dismissive comment and hoped the subject would be dropped. And it was. Except that Laura added that it might be diplomatic if they said nothing about Alexis Whitney to Karen's father. 'There's no point in antagonizing him unnecessarily,' she had supplemented ruefully. 'He thinks a lot of Ray and I don't think he'd encourage either of you to get involved with the Whitneys.'

And so that morning they had left Wakeley before ten and driven the two hundred miles to Maidenhead. It had not been a comfortable journey for Karen, neither physically nor mentally, conscious as only she was of the undercurrents here. Only really Shirley out of the four of them seemed totally relaxed, and Karen thought rather enviously that it was easy for her. So far as Shirley was concerned she had been invited to Alexis's home for the week-end to make up a foursome with Karen and Ray, and if she sometimes looked at Karen in a rather strange way that was only to be expected in the circumstances. Up until then she had believed Karen's relationship with Alexis to be a big secret, and to discover that Ray apparently knew all about it was rather disappointing. Nevertheless, the prospect of a week-end with nothing to do but enjoy herself provided a more than adequate compensation.

Alexis brought the big car to a halt at the foot of a flight of steps leading up to the main door. And almost as though on cue the door opened and a manservant appeared.

'Jeeves, I presume,' murmured Shirley with a giggle, and Alexis glanced round at her.

'Searle,' he corrected her with a smile. 'But he serves the same purpose.'

Shirley glowed under his attention, but then he thrust open his door and slid out, calling a greeting to the elderly man waiting on the steps.

As Karen had been seated behind Ray it was he who helped her out before going to help Alexis take their luggage out of the boot. She looked about her with undisguised interest. For all they were so near London it was very peaceful here, only the sounds of the river disturbing the stillness. She walked across a smooth lawn, looking towards the water, scarcely conscious of the others behind her. On the journey down Alexis had told them that his father had bought this house when he was only about ten years old, and she wondered what kind of a boy he had been then. Of course, his mother had been alive in those days, and no doubt she had spoiled him terribly. Mothers usually did. Particularly if their sons were as charming and attractive as Alexis.

A hand descended on her arm and she almost jumped out of her skin. It was Alexis and he was looking down at her with a curiously guarded expression in his eyes.

'Come along,' he said. 'We're waiting for you.'

Karen inclined her head in assent, but then with stumbling nervousness, she said: 'Am I – that is – are you going to introduce me to your parents as – as your fiancée?'

Alexis considered. 'Don't you think I should?'

'I don't know.' Karen was impatient. 'You must know what you intend to do.'

'Oh, yes.' He was mocking. 'I know that.'

'Well then?'

He shrugged. 'All right. Of course. That's the whole point of this exercise, isn't it?'

Karen frowned. 'But Shirley – what will she think?'

Alexis drew her determinedly back towards the steps where both Shirley and Ray were watching them with varying degrees of annoyance. 'Leave everything to me,' he remarked quietly, and then released her to take the steps two at a time after Searle.

In the hall they shed their coats and Alexis suggested that it might be best if they were shown their rooms first so that they could freshen up after the journey.

'What about lunch, sir?' inquired Searle politely. 'Have you eaten?'

'Thank you, yes. We stopped just outside of town and had a meal,' answered Alexis smoothly. 'Unless,' he glanced at the others, 'unless anyone would like some more coffee, or tea, perhaps.'

'Nothing for me, thanks,' answered Shirley, rubbing her stomach meaningfully. 'We had a delicious meal, didn't we?'

Searle looked relieved. 'I'm so glad, miss. What with the arrangements for the dinner party this evening, Cook's quite run off her feet.'

'I thought she might be,' commented Alexis, with a smile. 'Where is my father and his wife?'

'Mrs. Whitney's resting, I believe, sir, but your father's down at the boathouse, as far as I am aware.'

'I see.' Alexis nodded. Then he looked at his guests. 'I suggest you allow Searle to show you your rooms, and if you come down later, say about four, tea will be served in the lounge. Searle will tell you where that is.'

Ray ran a finger round the inside of his collar as though it was too tight for him. 'I could use a wash myself,' he said.

'Good.'

Alexis's eyes flickered over all of them, coming to rest for several seconds on Karen before he nodded politely and left them, walking across the hall and disappearing along a passage which appeared to lead to the back of the house. Karen thought he was probably going to the boathouse, to find his father. Why? To warn him of what to expect, perhaps?

But she wasn't given any time to speculate upon Alexis's movements. Just as Searle was about to show them the way upstairs, four people appeared at the top of the stairs on their way down, and the old manservant stood aside courteously.

There were two men and two women, probably married couples, Karen decided, in their late thirties, all dressed in tennis clothes. They smiled at Searle, but looked rather curiously at the others, and Karen wondered whether they were comparing the quality of their clothes with the expensively cut gear they were wearing.

After the others had gone and they were going upstairs, Shirley said: 'Who were they?' to a rather startled Searle. He was obviously not used to such impertinent questions.

'Why – er – some guests of Mr. Whitney's, miss,' he replied, and with that Shirley had to be content.

Their rooms were on the second floor, and Karen and Shirley were to share a bathroom, with Ray a little further along the corridor. For all that these rooms could not be used very frequently, they were beautifully decorated and furnished, and Shirley kept coming through their mutual bathroom into Karen's bedroom to exclaim at some new extravagance she had discovered. Karen herself wasn't particularly interested in her room. Instead, she walked to the long windows and perching on the seat looked down on the stretch of river spread out below her. From here it was possible to see the whole of the rear part of the building, and across the expanse of water the wooded slopes and rolling parkland of some unidentified common.

The Whitneys' property was extensive, with lots of trees and trellises, ideal hiding places for children. She could see an empty swimming pool, and some tennis courts on which the four people they had seen earlier were knocking a ball about. Lower, terraces gave on to wide shallow steps where the corrugated roof of a building which she suspected was the boathouse could be seen. And even as she watched, Alexis came out of the boat-house and up the steps accompanied by a tall, powerfully built man whom Karen vaguely recognized as Howard Whitney.

They came up the path together, stopping by the tennis courts to have a casual word with their visitors, and then disappeared under the lee of the building. Karen sighed. What would his father's reaction to their sup-posed engagement be? No doubt he would ultimately want someone better for his son, someone whose family could provide prestige and capital, or perhaps possess a title of their own. It was hinted that Howard Whitney expected a knighthood in the very near future. Certainly he would not look kindly on a girl whose father worked in the Wakeley mill, and who could offer nothing but her-self.

With an impatient gesture she got to her feet. What was she thinking of, speculating about such things? It didn't matter what the Whitneys thought of her. Sooner or later this assumed engagement would be broken and then she would make sure that she did not get involved with Alexis again.

Shirley came into the room dressed only in her slip, a towel about her bare shoulders. 'I'm going to take a shower,' she said. 'You don't mind?'

'Of course not.' Karen forced a light note into her voice.

Shirley watched her closely. 'This is a turn-up for the book, isn't it?'

'What?' Karen pretended ignorance.

'Why – coming here, of course.' She shook her head. 'I didn't realize Alexis had found me so attractive.'

'What do you mean?'

'Well, it's obvious, isn't it? Short of making some excuse to come to the school again there was no other way he could arrange things.'

'No. No, I suppose not.' Karen bent her head. 'Anyway, I expect there'll be dozens of guests.'

'Yes. Isn't it exciting!' Shirley raised her shoulders in an anticipatory gesture. 'I can't wait. What are you wearing? I've bought myself a new dress. It's sort of jungle printed, you know the sort of thing. Anyway, it suits me, or at least I think it does.'

Karen sat down at the dressing-table and studied her reflection critically. 'Oh, well I didn't buy a new dress. Just a blouse. I've brought a long skirt and I thought I could wear them together.'

Shirley nodded, not particularly interested. She was too absorbed with the prospect of stunning the men with her own brand of sophistication. With a little smile, she danced back into the bathroom, closing the door and sliding the bolt into place, and a few minutes later Karen heard the sound of water running.

Her case had been left at the foot of her bed and getting up now Karen began to unpack it. Capacious wardrobes were fitted against the walls and she opened the louvre doors and found dozens of coathangers. Then she took out her toilet bag and crossing to the pale blue wash-basin sluiced her face in cold water. She was drying her hands when there was a knock at her door and she called: 'Come in!' expecting it to be either Ray or one of the servants.

But it was Alexis who entered the room at her request, and she stood rather nervously looking at him, wondering what on earth he had come for. She was supremely conscious of her make-upless face and unsophisticated appearance, and wished she had had the sense to ask who it was before calling admittance.

Alexis was still wearing the cream suit he had worn to travel in, and now he said: 'My father wants to meet you. I've been asked to bring you down.' He glanced round the room with a tightening of his lips. 'Have you unpacked?'

'Why – why, yes. Does it matter?'

'No. Except that Searle will have to arrange to have all your things transferred to another room.'

'But why?' Karen was aghast.

'My fiancée should not be accommodated on the top floor. Now – are you ready?'

'No. No, I'm not. And I don't want to be moved either.' Karen stiffened her shoulders. 'I don't know anyone here but Ray and Shirley. I'd rather stay near them.'

'You know me!' remarked Alexis briefly.

'That's not – the same.'

'Why not?'

'Oh, you know why not!' she exclaimed. Then with trembling fingers she extracted her lipstick and eye-shadow from her handbag. 'Look, will you get out of here while I put on some make-up? I can't go to meet your father looking like this.'

Alexis folded his arms. 'You look all right to me.'

Karen shook her head and ignored him, leaning near to the dressing-table mirror to apply the eyeshadow to her lids. To her annoyance he remained where he was, watching her, and she had to force her hands not to shake as she applied the lipstick. Then she brushed her hair vigorously, allowing it to fall thickly and smoothly about her shoulders. She had not changed from the corded pants and balloon-sleeved red blouse she had worn to travel in, but at least she felt fresh again.

'I – I'm ready,' she said at last, and he stood aside to allow her to precede him out of the door.

It was just after three-thirty as he leant past her to push open the door of his father's study and then stood back to allow her to go first.

The impressive leather-tooled walls of the room were a fleeting impression as Karen met the penetrating brown eyes of Alexis's father. He rose, big and dominating, from behind his desk as they entered, and something inside her shrank from the piercing quality of those eyes. But to her surprise, the expression in their depths was not at all intimidating, and Howard came towards her smilingly, holding out his hand.

'Well, well,' he said tolerantly, looking beyond her for a moment to his son. 'So you're Dan Sinclair's daughter!'

Karen glanced round quickly at Alexis and then nodded, allowing Howard to take her hand, engulfing it in one of his. 'Yes,' she said. 'How do you do, Mr. Whitney?'

Howard chuckled. 'My word,' he said, in that same tolerant manner, 'I'm proud of you, lass, I really am.'

Karen was perplexed. She didn't know how to reply to him and Alexis came forward then, putting a casual arm across her shoulders in a familiar gesture.

'What my father means is that he never believed I'd ever settle down to matrimony,' he said. 'In his eyes, you've achieved the impossible.'

From his lazy, relaxed manner Karen could almost believe that this was really happening, that Alexis had actually asked her to marry him, that his father was really congratulating her for having accomplished something remarkable. She had to force herself to remember that this was just a charade to him, being played for the benefit of his stepmother. But that still left the question of her father. What if Howard Whitney took it into his head to telephone him about it? Her stomach seemed suddenly filled with butterflies.

'Never mind about that,' Howard was saying now, letting go of her hand with reluctance. 'Karen, isn't it? Well, let me say straight away how happy I am that Alex has decided to settle down at last, and that he's shown sense in choosing a wife. Never did care for these flibbertygibbet socialites he's been running around with these past few years! A Yorkshire lass I chose, and dammit, he's chosen one, too. I'm delighted!'

Karen was overwhelmed. She had expected coldness and recriminations, hostility barely disguised behind civility, but not this warmth and enthusiasm, this feeling of genuine pleasure.

'I – it's very kind of you,' she began, and then looked helplessly at Alexis.

'I've explained that you haven't told your father yet,' he remarked, his eyes holding hers. 'It's all been so sudden we haven't had much time to ourselves yet, have we?'

'Oh! Oh, no. That's right.' Karen swallowed convulsively. 'We – we thought we'd keep it a secret a little bit longer.'

'Well, I don't see why,' exclaimed Howard, shaking his head. 'By God, I'd like to announce it at the party this evening!'

'But you won't,' said Alexis, very definitely, and Howard acquiesced.

'No,' he agreed with a heavy sigh. 'No, I won't. But you've got to admit, Alex, sending you up to Wakeley was the best thing I ever did.'

Alexis allowed his arm to fall from Karen's shoulders and she felt suddenly cold. 'You could be right,' he remarked, going forward to help himself to a cigar from the box on Howard's desk.

'Never mind. This warrants a drink,' went on his father. 'Something celebratory. I know – we'll have a bottle of that champagne Searle's got put away for this evening.'

'Oh, really—' began Karen, feeling terrible, but the look in Alexis's tawny eyes squashed her protest at birth.

Howard walked to the study door and throwing it open, called 'Searle!' at the top of his voice. When the elderly manservant appeared Howard issued his orders without explanation, and Searle raised his grey eyebrows before going to do his master's bidding.

Howard closed the door again, rubbing his hands together delightedly, but the sound of his voice must have disturbed his wife, or perhaps she had already been on her way downstairs, Karen couldn't be certain; at any rate, before Searle could return with the champagne, the study door opened and Michelle Whitney appeared. She was wearing a pink silk gown, a sort of dressing-gown, Karen supposed, edged with ostrich feathers; the kind of gown Karen had hitherto not seen outside of the cinema screen, and she entered the room negligently, saying: 'Darling, must you always shout?'

As though becoming aware that her husband was not alone, her gaze drifted languidly round the room then, resting momentarily on Karen before shifting on to Alexis and her husband. With a faint inclination of her head, she signified her recognition of Alexis's presence, and then she went on: 'What's going on?'

Howard came forward and took her strongly by the shoulders. 'Michelle! I'm glad you've come down. We've certainly got something to celebrate now. Alex has got himself engaged. Isn't that wonderful news?'

Michelle shook herself free of her husband's heavy hands with delicate skill, a smile curving her lips but not, Karen saw, reaching her narrowed eyes. 'Really,' she said, assuming surprise. 'And to whom is he engaged?'

Howard turned to Karen, who had stiffened almost involuntarily. 'To Karen. Karen Sinclair. Her father is sub-manager of the Wakeley mill.' He chuckled, unable to hide his enthusiasm. 'Karen, allow me to introduce Alexis's stepmother, my wife Michelle.'

Karen held out her hand and it was enfolded for a fleeting moment in the other woman's. But the touch was limp and superficial and Karen was glad to be free again. Michelle herself seemed to be considering how best to respond to this news, and at last she said: 'Well, it's certainly a surprise, at any rate.' Her eyes flickered to Alexis. 'I suppose I should congratulate you, Alex, isn't that the usual form? But quite honestly I feel like congratulating Miss Sinclair, even if such congratulations are perhaps a little premature.'

Howard's beetling brows drew together. The insinuative undertones in his wife's voice were not lost on him, and he glanced uneasily at his son. Alexis for his part remained remarkably cool.

'I think a woman should always be congratulated,' he remarked mockingly. 'Actually getting her quarry down the aisle denotes the determination of the species. As you should know, Michelle.'

Hot colour ran up Michelle's cheeks at the implied insult, but Howard intervened by saying: 'At any rate, this is just between the four of us, for the time being. Karen hasn't told her parents yet, so let's keep it to ourselves, eh, Michelle?'

Michelle's lip curled, but at that moment. Searle returned with the champagne, and in the confusion of getting out glasses and drinking toasts the possible confrontation which had threatened was avoided.

Karen drank her champagne without enjoyment. The bubbles tickled her nose, but it was not a taste she had ever thought she could acquire. And right now she was too concerned with the impossibilities of her position to enjoy anything. She marvelled at Alexis's coolness and detachment. But then perhaps he was used to this kind of thing. She was not.

While they were drinking the champagne, the door opened and several people spilled into the room. They were obviously more of the guests, for they assumed that the champagne was in honour of Howard and Michelle and there was much laughter and comment which Karen felt completely apart from. Michelle, of course, basked in this concentrated attention, clearly considering this was her metier. Occasionally, Karen caught her sending little malicious glances in Alexis's direction, but if he was aware of them he gave no sign. Karen for her part withdrew into a corner, wishing there was some way of escape without pushing through the throng of people by the open doors.

She had thought Alexis engulfed by the group, but she was surprised suddenly to find him by her side. 'What's wrong?' he inquired lazily. 'Is it too much for you?'

Karen looked down at her half empty glass. 'Well, I'm not very keen on champagne,' she said.

'I didn't mean the champagne, and you know it,' he retorted. 'Do you want to get out of here?'

'Could I?' Karen stared at him.

'Of course. Come on.'

Giving her a moment to get rid of her glass, he took her hand within his strong hard fingers. Karen liked the sensations this contact aroused in her, but then she was being drawn with determination through the group of guests as Alexis threaded his way towards the door. He answered the many words of greeting addressed to him with merely a smile or a brief comment, and she wondered what his father's guests would think of their host's son deserting the celebrations. But she did catch sight of Howard's face and found no dissension there. On the contrary, he was wearing quite a complacent look and she realized he was imagining they wanted to be alone together.

In the hall, Alexis halted, but retained his hold on her hand. 'Would you like to see the grounds?' he suggested casually, and with a trembling awareness of what she was doing, Karen agreed. It was after four o'clock. Perhaps Ray and Shirley were even now in the lounge, wherever that might be, having tea. She ought to join them, but . . .

'It's this way,' said Alexis, and they walked down the passage he had followed earlier.

Half-way along the passage Alexis halted at double doors and releasing Karen pushed them open. Then he stood back to allow her to precede him into an enormous room. They were standing at one end, and a polished floor stretched ahead of them, gleaming warmly. It was a ballroom, she supposed, although it could have several uses. Only half the area was an integral part of the main building, the rest being a kind of built-on conservatory, with glass screens which had been folded back to increase the space available. Just now, several white-coated attendants were busily arranging flowers round a small dais, which would no doubt accommodate a band later, and putting finishing touches to the decorations. A looped net overhead contained scores of balloons and Karen could quite imagine their effectiveness in the muted lighting which would be used after dark.

Aware of Alexis watching her, she said: 'I've never been in a house with its own ballroom before.'

'Actually it was once a music room,' remarked Alexis, folding his arms, standing feet astride, surveying the scene. 'The glass-roofed extension was built by my father when my mother was alive. She loved plants and it was a veritable hothouse out there.'

Karen listened with interest. It was seldom he spoke about his own mother.

'Right. Shall we go?' He allowed his arms to fall to his sides and Karen nodded. She preceded him into the corridor again, and he closed the doors securely before slipping his hand beneath her elbow. 'It's a pity it's not summer,' he went on as they walked towards glass doors which gave on to a patio. 'We could have used the pool. You do swim, don't you?'

Karen nodded, and then they were outside in the cooling sunshine, but she didn't feel the cold. They crossed the tiled patio, went down some steps and passed the drained swimming pool. She thought there was nothing so depressing as an empty swimming pool and said so to Alexis.

He half smiled at this. 'Would you have it full to either freeze and splinter, or simply get clogged with dead leaves?'

Karen shook her head. 'I know it has to be emptied, but it seems so – so deserted, somehow.'

'I know what you mean.' His fingers on her elbow tightened imperceptibly. 'But at this time of the year one goes to the Bahamas to swim.'

Karen found herself wrinkling her nose at him. 'And what if one can't afford the Bahamas?'

'The swimming baths?' he suggested mockingly, and she laughed.

Suddenly there was an easy intimacy in their association that had not been there before; at least, not for seven years. She found herself talking to him quite naturally, telling him anecdotes about her pupils at school, listening while he regaled her with stories of his own escapades at boarding-school. They walked round the grounds, they sat for a few minutes on the steps leading down to the boathouse just looking at the river, and then retraced their steps to enter a small summer pavilion that Alexis said he and his friends had used for various purposes in their games as children. It had been a school and a hospital, a ship at sea, and a desert island, and sometimes even a stagecoach being attacked by Indians.

When they finally walked back to the house Karen felt a stab of regret which was further increased when Ray met them in the hall and demanded to know where they had been.

'Do you realize it's almost five-thirty?' he asked, aggressively, so that Alexis said: 'Keep your voice down,' in a warning tone.

'Why should I?' Ray was angry. 'You told us we'd have tea in the lounge at four o'clock—'

'And didn't you?'

'Shirley and I did, yes.'

'Well?'

'We expected you to join us; Karen, anyway.'

Karen sighed. 'I'm sorry, Ray. It was my fault. I asked – Alexis to show me the grounds.'

Ray thrust his hands into his trousers pockets. 'We'd all have liked to see the grounds,' he muttered. 'Instead of sitting in there,' he jerked his head behind him, 'drinking cups of tea!'

Alexis made a calming gesture. 'Let's not get hysterical about it,' he remarked briefly. 'Do you want some tea now, Karen?'

Karen shook her head. 'No, thanks. I – I'm not hungry – or thirsty either.'

Ray sniffed. 'What time's this party supposed to begin?'

'Dinner's at eight,' replied Alexis, glancing at his watch. 'We usually have a drink before the meal – say about half past seven.'

'And what am I supposed to do until then?' Ray was peevish.

Alexis shrugged. 'Whatever you like. We have a kind of snooker-room in the basement. Searle will show you. And now I'd better go and find my father. There are some business matters which require his attention. I'll see you – all – later.'

After he had left them, Karen looked rather apprehensively at Ray. 'I'm sorry,' she said again. 'Where is Shirley?'

Now it was Ray's turn to look uncomfortable. 'I – er – she's in her room, I think.'

'You think?' Karen frowned. 'Don't you know?'

'No.' Ray was belligerent. 'Do you feel like a game of snooker?'

'I don't play.' Karen looked at him curiously. 'What's wrong? Have you and Shirley had a row or something?'

'A row?' He gave an indignant snort. 'Of course we haven't had a row.'

Karen rubbed her nose. 'I only asked,' she remarked dryly.

Ray sighed. 'What are you going to do now?'

'I thought I might go up to my room, too. There doesn't seem much else to do, does there? I mean, we don't know anyone, do we?'

Ray scuffed his toe. 'You go on. I think I'll have a look downstairs if I can find someone to show me the way. See you at the reception!' His tone was dry.

'All right, Ray.' Karen managed a smile and then began climbing the stairs. Half-way up she wondered with trepidation whether against her will Alexis had had her things moved to another room, but she was relieved to find everything as she had left it. She flung herself on the bed without bothering to take off her clothes and stared moodily up at the ceiling. What was the matter with her? Why was she feeling so depressed suddenly? Fifteen minutes ago she had been almost happy.

There was a tap on her door and she propped herself up on her elbows nervously, hardly daring to call come in. But then she realized that the tap had been on the bathroom door, and presently a voice called: 'Karen! Karen, is that you?'

With a sigh, she answered: 'Yes, Shirley, it's me. Come on in.'

Shirley came into the room wearing an attractive, close-fitting dress of apricot jersey which moulded the curves of her figure and showed a long length of leg. But her make-up was smudged and she didn't look at all happy.

Karen frowned. 'Hello,' she said. 'Are you all right?'

Shirley raised her plucked eyebrows. 'I guess so.' Then she turned to the other girl. 'Where were you? We had tea ages ago.'

Karen swung her legs to the floor. 'Alexis showed me the grounds.'

'You? Why you?'

'I asked him to,' said Karen carefully.

Shirley digested this. Then she said without warning: 'It's you he's interested in, isn't it? Not me at all.'

Karen flushed. 'Why do you say a thing like that?'

'Oh, I just know.' Shirley tugged the handkerchief that she was carrying between her fingers. 'I just want to know why I'm here, that's all.'

'Oh, Shirley—'

'Oh, Shirley, nothing! I'm here to put up a smoke screen, aren't I? To make Ray think it's me he's interested in when it's you all the time—'

'It's not like that at all!'

'Then what is it like? I have a right to know.'

Karen bent her head. 'Alexis is not interested in either of us.'

Shirley stared at her incredulously. 'Don't give me that!'

'It's the truth! He – well, he wouldn't be interested in girls like us, would he? Be honest! Can you see someone like him really troubling about girls from a provincial Yorkshire town when he can have his pick of almost anyone?'

'Then why are we here?' Shirley stared at her.

'Because – because of his stepmother.'

'Do you know her?'

'Not exactly. I have met her, though.'

'And?'

148

'Well, it's a long story, Shirley. Can't you just accept that our being here serves the purpose and enjoy the week-end for what it is?'

Shirley paced restlessly about the room. 'There's still Ray.'

'What about Ray?' Karen looked up.

Shirley halted and looked down at the fraying handkerchief. 'Does he know why we're here?'

'Of course.'

Shirley shook her head. 'He didn't tell me.'

'Why should he?' Karen was curious.

Shirley looked at her then with ravaged eyes. 'Can't you guess?'

'No.' Karen was confused. 'What's there to guess?'

Shirley sniffed petulantly. 'He was angry when you didn't come for tea. There was only the two of us in that huge lounge! Have you seen it?' Karen shook her head and Shirley went on: 'He guessed you'd gone off with Alexis, I suppose, but I didn't.'

Karen got to her feet. The suspicion of what Shirley was trying to say was beginning to germinate in her mind. 'Are you trying to tell me that Ray is responsible for – for your being so distrait?' she asked quietly.

Shirley shredded the handkerchief. 'Oh, yes, yes!' She caught her breath on a sob. 'I thought he liked me, I was sure he did. But – but—'

'But what?' Karen was growing impatient.

Shirley's mouth worked. 'He was so angry after-wards—'

'After what?' Karen felt amazingly calm in the circumstances.

'After he kissed me, of course.' Shirley sniffed again. 'I – I have to tell you, Karen. There's no one else.'

Karen wished she smoked. A cigarette would have cooled her down. 'But why should you imagine he doesn't like you?' she asked. 'If he – kissed you—'

'It was what he said – about you and Alexis Whitney.

He was just using me to get back at you!'

'Did he actually say that?'

'Not in so many words, but I knew!' Shirley drew a shaking breath. 'He was so angry!'

'Oh, Shirley!'

Karen didn't know what to say. She supposed she should be feeling resentful herself and angry, too, that Ray should attempt to make love to another girl behind her back, but she wasn't. She just felt indifferent, detached. It was all wrong. Everything was wrong!

'I shouldn't have come,' Shirley was berating herself now, pacing up and down once more. 'I don't want to be responsible for splitting you two up.'

Karen shook her head. 'Please, Shirley, don't get upset about it. Maybe if Ray so easily turns to another woman behind my back it's time we were split up, as you put it.'

'I've told you. He was angry, that's all.'

'Men don't kiss women they're not attracted to, just because they're angry,' Karen pointed out dryly. 'However, I wouldn't presume to judge what Ray's motives might be.'

Shirley hunched her shoulders. 'I always thought he liked me,' she said again, almost to herself.

Karen, who had been about to turn away, looked back at her. 'I didn't know you knew him that well.'

Shirley flushed now. 'I don't – not really. But sometimes on Friday evenings . . .' She paused.

'Yes?' Karen was curious in spite of herself. 'What about Friday evenings?'

Shirley caught her lower lip between her teeth. 'You know Ray is always late on Friday evenings, because of the choir practice? Well, I sometimes work late on Fridays, too.'

'I see. Go on.'

'Well, sometimes he gives me a lift, just into town, you understand. And a couple of times we've had a drink together.'

'Have you? Have you really?'

All of a sudden Karen did feel angry. Ray had been so indignant when he had accused her of going out with Alexis behind his back, but never once had he told her that he knew Shirley Scott in any other way than as the headmaster's secretary.

'Are – are you going to tell him I've told you?' Shirley sounded anxious.

'Not unless I have to. Did he tell you not to tell me?'

'No. No, but it was sort of taken for granted.'

'I'll bet it was!' Karen tugged angrily at a strand of her dark hair. Then realizing that time was passing and she still needed a bath, she said: 'Just leave it, Shirley, shall we? There's no point in causing any more trouble. At least not here.'

Shirley nodded reluctantly. 'I'm not looking forward to it at all now.'

'Nor am I,' remarked Karen grimly, beginning to unbutton her blouse. With so many complications, how could she enjoy anything?

CHAPTER TEN

KAREN's skirt was made of corded velvet and was the colour of amethysts. The blouse she had bought to wear with it was white and made of lace, with sleeves that clung to her upper arms, ballooned out over her forearms, and were gathered in a broad cuff at her wrists. The neckline was low and round, showing the creamy swell of her breasts. She had brushed her hair until it shone, swinging thickly against her cheeks, while the silver hoops she had worn the night of the Summertons' dinner party glinted in her ears. She was making a final examination of her face in the mirror when Ray knocked at her door.

He came in at her invitation looking slightly stiff and uncomfortable in a dinner suit. 'Are you ready?' he asked, and she nodded. 'You look beautiful,' he added. 'You suit long skirts. Some women aren't tall enough.'

'Thank you.' Karen picked up her sequinned purse. 'Where's Shirley?'

'Next door, I suppose. Haven't you seen her?'

'Yes, I've seen her. ' Karen watched Ray's face closely and observed the guarded expression which entered his eyes. 'Perhaps you'd better give her a knock, too.'

Ray hesitated, obviously undecided as to whether to behave normally or to confide that he and Shirley had had a row. Choosing the former, he walked back along the corridor to her door and knocked. Karen heard the door being opened and words being exchanged, and then Ray came back again, his face flushed.

'She says she's not going down,' he said. 'She says she has a headache.'

'Oh, no!' Karen brushed past him and made her own way to Shirley's door. Opening it, she looked inside and found the other girl stretched out on her bed, still in a dressing-gown. 'Shirley! Come on! There's to be dancing later. You like dancing, don't you?'

'I've got a headache,' said Shirley, in a muffled voice, her arm resting across her eyes. 'Just go away and leave me alone.'

Karen would have liked to have said more, but Ray looked significantly at his watch and with a sigh she closed the door again and turned to him. 'You know what's wrong with her, don't you?' she challenged him.

'How should I know?'

'Because you're responsible!' Karen made an impatient gesture. 'Oh, it's no good arguing about it now. We'll talk about it later.'

Ray didn't make any comment and in silence they descended the stairs. The reception was to be held in the huge lounge where Ray and Shirley had been earlier, but as they reached the first landing they could see that the hall was thronged with people, too, all laughing and talking together and helping themselves liberally from the trays of drinks being circulated amongst them by a veritable army of white-coated attendants.

Ray heaved a sigh. 'God,' he muttered. 'Where are they all going to eat dinner?'

Karen raised her shoulders helplessly, less concerned with food than with her own part in this. She searched the assembled guests in an effort to see one familiar face, albeit that of Michelle, when a voice behind them said: 'Don't let them intimidate you. A crowd is only a collection of individuals.'

Karen turned in relief to find Alexis behind them looking disturbingly attractive in his dinner clothes. Unlike Ray he wore them with ease, the narrow trousers accentuating the muscular strength of his legs.

'Shirley's not coming down,' she said quickly. 'She's – er – got a headache.'

'Oh, really?' Alexis's eyes narrowed. 'She was all right this afternoon, wasn't she?'

'I expect it was the car journey,' remarked Ray stiffly. 'Some people are not good travellers.'

Karen cast an interrogative glance in his direction, but he looked away, and apparently unaware of this little interchange, Alexis said: 'Shall we go down? I can see some friends of mine over there I'd like you to meet.'

The next half hour was filled with unfamiliar faces making unfamiliar conversations. Karen drank several Martini cocktails, gave noncommittal answers to personal questions, and stayed beside Alexis almost as though he was her lifeline in a stormy sea.

Ray remained with them, dour and taciturn, clearly not enjoying himself at all. But he drank rather freely and Karen found herself hoping that the food would be served soon. Once the actual dinner was over and dancing began they might be able to escape.

Dinner was eventually served upstairs in the room which Karen assumed was over the ballroom downstairs. There was a long table at which she was expected to sit with Alexis and his father and stepmother, and two other tables set at right angles to this which accommodated the other guests. In consequence Karen was separated from Ray, but after she was seated beside Alexis, with someone called Alan Forster on her right, she was relieved to see that he appeared to be talking to a young woman sitting beside him. Camera bulbs flashed as the scene was recorded for the local paper, and Karen hoped that it would not be important enough to get into the national press. It seemed unlikely, and in any case she was only another guest, a shadowy outline on a photograph of Mr. and Mrs. Howard Whitney.

When the meal was served Alexis turned to her. 'Are you finding it all rather a bore?' he asked in a low tone.

Karen looked at him. 'Why do you ask?'

He shrugged. 'I don't know. You looked rather tense earlier on. I thought you were wishing you hadn't agreed to come.'

'I've already wished that,' replied Karen tersely, beginning to eat her prawn cocktail.

'Why?' Alexis spooned prawns and mayonnaise into his mouth. 'Is it something I've done particularly?'

Karen had to be honest. 'Well, asking us here was something you've done,' she answered, with a sigh.

'I thought you were enjoying yourself this afternoon.'

'When?' She was deliberately obtuse.

'You know when,' he insisted softly. 'When we were talking in the grounds.'

Karen had had enough of her cocktail suddenly and pushed it aside. 'I – I did enjoy it,' she admitted, taking a sip of her wine. 'But this is something else.'

'Why? I'm here, aren't I?'

She bent her head. 'For how much longer, I wonder.'

'Why do you say that?'

'I've no doubt, when the dancing begins, your vigil will be over. From the killing glances I've received from certain quarters, I should think my presence here isn't altogether appreciated.'

He half smiled. 'I shouldn't have thought that would worry you one way or the other. If I leave, you'll have Ray all to yourself.'

Karen's hands curled tightly on her lap. Was he baiting her, or was he aware of the conflict between them? She couldn't be sure, and she glanced at him uneasily.

Alexis caught that glance and dropping his hand from the table he sought hers, clenched in her lap. Prising them apart, he allowed his fingers to play with hers, watching her all the while until she was forced to look away. Determinedly, she drew her hands back to rest on the edge of the table and he turned his attention to his wine.

The meal progressed slowly through eight courses with coffee and liqueurs to finish. Alexis's father, who was seated on his other side, had attracted his son's attention half-way through the meal with some talk of a fault in the engine of the power boat they kept in the boathouse, and Karen told herself she was relieved. But for all the anxieties she suffered when Alexis was baiting her she still found his company more stimulating than any other man she had ever met, and she found herself listening to everything he said with an increasing fervour.

At last the meal was over, toasts to the anniversary couple were made and answered, and everyone began to leave the tables and make their way downstairs again to the ballroom from where the sounds of music were already beginning to drift.

Alexis held Karen's chair for her and then in the company of his father and stepmother and several other couples they made their way downstairs, too. It was very warm, or perhaps it was the amount of wine she had consumed, Karen could not be sure, but certainly she felt as though her limbs were burning.

Ray made his way towards them when they reached the long corridor leading to the music-room, and Alexis excused himself to attend to some details for his father.

'Well?' said Ray, looking round. 'Enjoying yourself?'

Karen shook her head. 'Are you?'

'You must be joking. This is not my scene, Karen. I feel out of place here. I'll be glad when it's all over.'

She was dancing with Ray when Alexis came back. She saw him immediately. Apart from the fact that he was tall, his pale hair was a brilliant identification in the muted lights. Ray saw him too and said: 'Have you seen the way that stepmother of Whitney's looks at him?'

Karen didn't want to listen. 'The band's good, isn't it?' she said, pretending not to have heard.

'She's not at all what I would have expected,' Ray went on, almost as though Karen had not spoken. 'I'm beginning to understand why Whitney thought she might try to cause trouble. If ever a woman had malice in mind ...'

Karen sighed. 'I don't want to talk about it.'

'I wonder why she married the old man if she's so keen on the son,' mused Ray thoughtfully

'Alexis wouldn't marry her,' retorted Karen, unable to prevent herself, and then coloured at the look in Ray's eyes.

'Really! And how do you know that?'

'Someone told me.' Karen was reluctant to reveal her source.

'Who? Whitney?'

'No, of course not.'

'Hmm.' Ray didn't sound convinced. 'Well, anyway, he was right. You don't marry women like that!'

'How do you know what she's like?' exclaimed Karen in surprise.

Ray shrugged. 'I don't know. Masculine instinct, I suppose. Women aren't the only ones to know things by instinct, you know.'

The five-piece band on the flower-banked dais finished the tune it was playing and they walked slowly off the floor. As they did so they almost bumped into Howard Whitney and his wife who were standing with a group of people talking. Howard turned to Karen at once and said: 'So there you are, my dear. I think Alex has been looking for you. But before he succeeds in finding you, you are going to have a dance with me, I hope.'

Karen managed a smile. 'I should be delighted,' she replied, glancing round at Ray. Then she met Michelle's appraising stare. 'Hello, Mrs. Whitney. It's a lovely party.'

Michelle looked speculatively at Ray. 'So glad you're enjoying yourselves,' she remarked, the slight slur in her voice giving evidence of the fact that she had already drunk more than was good for her. She put a casual hand on Ray's shoulder. 'And who are you? I haven't seen you before.'

Howard looked rather tense and Karen was embarrassed for him. She was unutterably relieved when the band struck up a waltz and he was able to draw her on to the floor to dance.

'Take no notice of Michelle, my dear,' he said apologetically. 'She can be rather provocative in this mood.'

'That's all right.' Karen wished he would just let it go.

'I'm so glad for you and Alex,' Howard went on, shifting from one precarious subject to another. 'I'm sure you'll be very happy together.'

'Thank you.'

He swung her round. 'I should have guessed, of course. Alex has been a different man since he went to Wakeley.'

'What do you mean?' Karen couldn't prevent the question.

'Well—' Howard sighed. 'Don't take this wrongly, but there have been – no women.' He looked down at her searchingly. 'In my experience, that only means one thing.'

Karen flushed. 'I don't understand.'

'Alex has been a bit of a tearaway.' Howard's brows drew together heavily. 'I suppose in some ways it's been my fault, but who can really be sure about a thing like that?'

'I don't think his past life is anything to do with me,' murmured Karen uncomfortably.

'No, maybe not. But just in case anyone takes it into their heads to tell you tales about him, I'd like to say something in his defence.'

Karen wondered who he was thinking about in this respect. Michelle, perhaps? It seemed he was not as blind to his wife's failings as Alexis imagined him to be.

'You see,' he went on, 'Alex's mother died eight years ago when he was just twenty-one. He was away at university at the time, and it was a terrible shock for him – for both of us.' He sighed. 'But at my age one accepts these things and realizes that life must go on. I'm afraid Alex found that harder to accept.'

'He's an only child,' said Karen quietly.

'Yes. Unfortunately. But Frances was never a strong woman, and having Alex nearly killed her.'

'I see.'

Howard shook his head. 'But it wasn't only his mother's death that – upset him. It was my remarriage that really sent him off the rails.' He heaved another sigh. 'Alex had known Michelle, you see. They'd been friends for about a year. She was a model and her work took her all over the country. For all he was at university, I believe they saw quite a lot of one another. But then Michelle met me and – well, I suppose we fell in love. She stopped seeing Alex and in six months we were married. Oh, I realize now it was too soon after his mother's death to put another woman in her place, but—' he made a helpless movement of his shoulders, 'these things happen. Alex had to accept it.' He frowned again. 'Of course for a time I got very bad reports from his tutors. I'm amazed he wasn't sent down. But gradually he seemed to realize that he needed his degree, and needless to say he got it. He has a good brain, don't let his attitude hide that from you. He always was an intelligent child. That was half his trouble.'

The music came to a stop and Howard looked down at her. 'Well?' he said. 'Have I helped you to understand your fiancé a little better?'

Karen's lips quivered. 'I – I think so.'

'Good. Now, let's go and have a drink together. Dancing makes me thirsty.'

'But – but – your wife. Ray—'

'They can take care of themselves. Come along. It's not every day I can buy my son's fiancée a drink.'

Karen was forced to go with him. Long tables had been set in the glass-fronted conservatory extension and Howard made his way to the nearest one. 'What will you have?' he asked. 'Champagne?'

'Oh, no – thank you. Er – could I just have a lime and lemon, please?'

Howard pursed his lips. 'Lime and lemon!' he exclaimed. He looked resignedly at the bartender. 'What would you do with her? All right, all right, lime and lemon it shall be. But put a dash of Scotch in it for good measure.'

Karen was half-way down her long glass of iced whisky, lime and lemon, when Alexis pushed his way past the group nearest to them and came to join them. His face was grim and he looked searchingly at his father before turning to Karen.

'Where the hell have you been?' he demanded. 'I've been looking everywhere for you.'

Karen opened her mouth to reply when Howard intervened. 'She's been dancing with me,' he said. 'You can't expect to keep her all to yourself, Alex.'

Alexis took a deep breath, calming himself. 'Perhaps you ought to go and look after Michelle,' he stated pointedly. 'She's swallowing gin like there was no tomorrow.'

Howard's lips tightened, but he finished his own Scotch and put his glass down on the table. 'Very well,' he said. He looked again at Karen. 'Excuse me, my dear. If I don't see you any more this evening, I shall expect to see you tomorrow before you leave.'

'All right.' Karen smiled, and watched as his tall, broad frame threaded its way down the hall to find Michelle. Then she looked at Alexis. 'You were rude,' she said. 'There was no need to be.'

Alexis's jaw hardened. 'Wasn't there? Exactly what has he been saying to you?'

Karen raised her dark eyebrows. 'He was just telling me a little about your mother.'

'And what else?'

'Nothing much.' Karen finished her drink. 'That was delicious. Do you think I could have another?'

'No, you're coming with me. I want to talk to you now.'

He took hold of her wrist and she had perforce to go with him. Either that or cause an unpleasant scene. But she resented his arrogance, his assumption that he had the right to command her movements. She was quite sure that several pairs of eyes followed their progress from the room, and no doubt Ray's were amongst them. Not that he would be likely to say anything, she thought rather scornfully. He had no doubt decided that his behaviour this week-end justified silence in such matters.

They followed the corridor to the hall where Alexis opened double doors into what appeared to be a library. He went ahead, switching on a lamp to disperse the gloom, and Karen followed him, reluctantly closing the doors behind her. Alexis walked straight over to the drinks cabinet and poured himself a stiff Scotch, swallowing it at a gulp, and Karen's eyes widened incredulously. Pouring another, he turned to face her, saying: 'What's wrong? Haven't you ever seen anyone swallow a drink before?'

'Not – not like that,' she admitted.

'No – well, I needed it,' he remarked heavily. Raising his glass to his lips again, he drank a little more and then putting it down said: 'Can I get you that drink now?'

'No, thanks.' Karen looked round. 'Why have you brought me here? What have you to say that couldn't be said in there?'

'Just this!' he said thickly, and before she could presage his actions he had covered the space between them and pulled her into his arms. He bent his head to hers, kissing her lips as she attempted to draw back, his hands on her hips, holding her against him. Once – twice, he kissed her, and she felt her lips parting involuntaily. Then he kissed her again, and this time he wasn't playing with her as he had been before; he was drawing the very strength from her body.

'Oh, Alexis!' she breathed weakly, her hands sliding up

to his hair, gripping handfuls of it to hold him closer.

And then the library door opened and Michelle stood on the threshold, swaying slightly, her gown of silk chiffon clinging about her legs. Karen would have dragged herself away from Alexis, but he would not let her go, and instead they all stared at one another for a long agonizing minute.

Karen expected her to say something, expected some verbal onslaught, some recriminatory abuse that never came. Instead, she turned again and left them, and now Karen felt as cold as ice. It was as though a chill wind had blown through the library, freezing her to the core.

She wrenched herself away from Alexis, and when his face darkened angrily and he reached for her again, she darted to the door and went out into the hall. She stood there for several minutes, breathing deeply, long uneven breaths that shook her slender frame. What was she doing allowing him to kiss her like that? Thank God Michelle had brought her to her senses before it was too late.

She felt someone behind her and swung round nervously to confront Alexis, shrinking at the cold anger in his eyes. 'Don't ever do that to me again!' he muttered harshly, but before she could reply there was a clamour from the ballroom and the sound of a fanfare being sounded.

Alexis frowned, and gripping her arm he urged her deliberately forward in the direction of the noise. They halted by the doors leading into the ballroom and over the heads of the people Karen could see Michelle climbing unsteadily on to the orchestra dais. She looked at Alexis and saw he was watching Michelle, too, a guarded expression in his eyes.

'Lad – ladies and gentlemen!' Michelle was having difficulty in articulating and now Karen could see the top of Howard's head as he stood by the dais, apparently appealing to his wife to get down.

'Ladies and gentlemen!'she said again, and the camera

bulbs flashed in her face, making her giggle uncontrollably for a few moments. 'I have an announ – announce – ment to make!' She straightened her shoulders. 'Something I'm sure you'll all want to hear.'

She looked straight across the room and Karen could have sworn she was looking at them. And suddenly she knew she was. Alexis knew it, too, and with a grim twist to his mouth he began pushing his way through the press of people towards the dais. But he didn't reach it before Michelle completed what she had begun to say.

'It concerns Alex – my stepson,' she went on, smiling maliciously. 'A real cause for celebration if ever there was one. Alex has got himself engaged! Isn't that exciting! To that sweet little Yorkshire girl he's been escorting this evening – Karen Sinclair!'

Karen turned before anyone could stop her and ran back along the corridor to the hall. The stairs had never seemed so long or so steep, but at last she reached the sanctuary of her room and closing the door leant back against it weakly.

Oh, she had been right to feel apprehensive. Michelle had been determined to cause trouble, even Ray had seen that. She must have guessed their subterfuge was for her benefit, and she would know, better even than Howard, that a man like Alexis Whitney wouldn't seriously consider marrying an insignificant nobody from Wakeley. Karen doubted he would ever marry anyone, unless it was for reasons of expediency, of course.

She stared miserably round the bedroom. She should never have agreed to come, she told herself again. She had only ever experienced heartache where Alexis Whitney was concerned, and she was a fool to go on inviting more. The idea of Michelle informing the Wakeley press that she had spent a night in Alexis's house didn't seem to matter much any more, and she wished she had had the courage to make a clean breast of it to her parents at the time. Then she wouldn't have been subject to this kind of moral blackmail.

Crossing the room, she seated herself at the dressing-table and stared wearily at her reflection. But it wasn't only what her parents would say that was troubling her now. It was also what had happened just before Michelle had made her startling announcement; it was that moment in the library when Alexis had kissed her and she had realized that she couldn't pretend to herself any more. The reason that Alexis could arouse her so easily, why he could destroy any defences she might raise against him was quite simple: she was in love with him . . .

She rose abruptly to her feet. If only her mother were there. If only there was someone she could talk to. Not necessarily about herself, but just to banish the misery from her mind.

And then she thought of Shirley.

Although they might have no great love for one another, at least they were from the same town, the same background, the same school, even. Perhaps Shirley might provide the solace she needed. She could tell her about the dance, about the dinner, although she shuddered at the thought of food.

Opening the bathroom door, she went through to Shirley's door and tapped lightly. 'Shirley! Shirley, are you awake?'

There was no reply, so she opened the door, the shaft of light from her bedroom penetrating the darkness beyond. And then her senses froze. Shirley was there, she was awake, but she wasn't alone. And the curly dark head beside her on the pillow was Ray's.

Karen was aghast. In spite of her newly discovered love for Alexis, she would never have expected this of Ray. He had not been like that. He had never made any attempt to make love to her. But now . . .

The light had disturbed them, but Karen didn't wait for them to speak. She slammed the door shut again and rushed through the bathroom to her own bedroom, trem-

164

bling uncontrollably.

It was too much, entirely too much. Closing her door, she stood for a moment hugging herself, trying to calm her shaken nerves. That Ray should treat her like this seemed totally incomprehensible, until she began to see that perhaps that was what had been wrong with their relationship all along. They had never felt like that about one another.

Straightening, she moved away from the door and stared hopelessly into space. What now? What was she going to do? What could she do?

As though in answer to her silent appeal there came a knocking on the outer door and she stiffened.

'Karen! Karen! I want to speak to you. Can I come in?'

On shaking legs she ran across the room and turned the key in the lock. Then she said: 'No. Go away, Alexis. I don't want to speak to anyone.'

'Karen, *please*!' There was grim demand in his voice. 'This is crazy! I want to speak to you – to explain—'

'Go away!' Karen pressed a hand to her lips. 'I've got nothing to say.'

There was silence for a long moment and she thought he had gone, but then he said in a calmer voice: 'Karen, open the door! I've got to talk to you.'

'I've already had one example of your way of talking this evening,' she replied huskily. 'Just go away! Tell your friends what you like, but go away!'

She heard his intake of breath, his muttered imprecation, and then the sound of his footsteps receding down the corridor. He had gone!

She visibly sagged, making her way to the bed and sinking down upon it wearily. What a mess, she thought, feeling slightly sick. However was she going to face them – any of them – in the morning? How could they all climb into Alexis's car and drive back as though nothing momentous had happened? It was impossible. And she for one couldn't and wouldn't do it.

She glanced at her watch. It was after midnight, but it would be hours yet before the party broke up. If she wanted to leave without being seen she would have to wait until they had all sought their beds, which could mean after breakfast. She sighed. What time would she be able to get a train to Leeds? Ten o'clock? Eleven o'clock? It was Sunday morning. What kind of a service could she expect?

She lay back on the bed and stared up at the ceiling. What did it matter? Sooner or later there would be a train, and she would be on it . . .

CHAPTER ELEVEN

THE train from King's Cross arrived at Leeds soon after one o'clock in the afternoon. Karen had been lucky enough to arrive at the station only minutes before its departure, and she had sunk down into her seat with a tremendous feeling of release.

Leaving Falcons had been comparatively easy, though.

By seven o'clock that morning, the house had been quiet, but she had waited another half hour before leaving her room. Half-way down the stairs she had seen Searle in the hall below, and had almost taken fright when he turned and saw her. But in fact, after ascertaining that she was leaving he had called a taxi for her, showing little surprise that she should go in this manner. Perhaps he was used to such little intrigues, Karen had thought unhappily.

She had not had a thing to eat since dinner the previous evening and by the time she left Leeds station she was feeling slightly sick. Reaction was playing its part, too, and now that she was actually back on her home ground, so to speak, she began wondering what sort of reaction her leaving would have on those she had left behind. No doubt Ray and Shirley would be relieved, she thought dryly, looking up and down the street. At least they would have time to compose themselves before meeting her again.

There was a bus to Wakeley at two o'clock, and in the interval she went into the bus station cafeteria and bought herself a cup of coffee and a ham roll. As she sat there trying to swallow the rather stodgy roll she endeavoured to collect her thoughts and put some coherence into what she was going to tell her parents.

She had decided to be honest with them and explain about the night she had spent at the house with Alexis. Her mother for one might support her, and surely if she assured her father that in future she intended to have nothing more to do with Alexis, he would not be too distressed.

She sighed. But it was going to be difficult. And there was still Ray and Shirley to consider. If only she was young again, she thought futilely. If only she could have left Wakeley altogether and gone to her aunt's in Keswick as she had done before. How much simpler life would be.

But one couldn't go on running away for ever, she realized, and although she did not regret leaving Falcons so precipitately, nevertheless, this had been another example of trying to escape from her own foolishness.

It began to rain as the bus neared Wakeley and by the time it set her down in the High Street it was pouring. She had not taken an overcoat with her, only a suède jacket she wore with her trousers, and this was hardly adequate covering in this downpour.

Hugging her case, she ran along the High Street to Norfolk Road, and then, out of breath with the weight of the suitcase, she plodded more slowly up the street to her parents' house.

When she entered the hallway, her mother came out of the living-room to see who it was, and gazed in consternation at Karen's soaked appearance.

'For heaven's sake!' she exclaimed. 'Where have you come from?'

Karen was shivering by now, and her teeth chattered as she tried to speak. 'I – I got off the bus – in – in the High Street. Gosh, I'm frozen!'

Laura Sinclair clicked her tongue impatiently. 'What were you doing getting off the bus in the High Street? I thought you were in London!'

The living-room door opened wider and Karen's father

appeared, the Sunday newspaper tucked under his arm. 'Good God!' he ejaculated. 'It's Karen!' His expression darkened angrily. 'What's been going on? Where've you been?' He gave his wife an accusing stare. 'Didn't I tell you, you should have told me before letting her go off with that scoundrel?'

Karen shivered uncontrollably, but she looked uncomprehendingly at her mother. 'Who – who does he mean?'

'Whitney, of course,' snapped her father, and her mother gave an expressive little shake of her head.

'I told your father last night,' she explained quietly. 'I thought it was best.'

Karen nodded. 'It – it was. Bu – but could I go and get these clothes off before either of you starts, because I – I'm so – so cold!'

Laura seemed to come to her senses and realized her daughter was visibly shrinking before her eyes. 'Of course, of course,' she said at once. 'Dan, go and put on the kettle while I help Karen off with these things.'

'But what about—'

'Later, Dan, later.' Laura squeezed his arm reassuringly and then indicated that Karen should lead the way upstairs.

In the bathroom, Karen stripped off all her clothes and her mother towelled her vigorously. Then she said: 'You know, I think you'd better get in the bath. Your skin's so cold. I'm afraid you may have caught a chill.'

Karen nodded, unable to stop shivering, and with an anxious expression on her face, her mother turned on the bath taps. Half an hour later, Karen had stopped shivering quite so convulsively, but she still couldn't get warm despite the warm pyjamas of her mother's she was wearing, and the enveloping folds of her father's dressing-gown.

She sat beside the fire downstairs, especially built up for her benefit, and sipped the tea her mother had made with real enjoyment. She felt mentally warm and cosseted, and ashamed that she had not been honest with her parents all along.

'Now,' said her father with obvious impatience, 'what were you doing getting off the bus in Wakeley? Haven't you been to London? Or didn't he bring you home?'

Karen took a deep breath. 'Yes, I've been to London, and yes, Alexis would have brought me home. At least, I suppose he would. But – but I didn't want to stay.'

'Why?' Her mother stared at her. 'Oh, Karen, he hasn't – I mean – you didn't—?'

'No, I didn't,' said Karen firmly. 'That wasn't why I came away.'

'Then why did you?' demanded her father.

Slowly and painstakingly, Karen explained that she had gone to see Alexis when he was ill, and that she had spent the night at the house. Her father would have interrupted her then, but her mother prevented him, raising her eyebrows warningly, conveying without words that anger would achieve nothing now.

When Karen got to the part about Michelle Whitney, however, even Laura could not remain silent, 'I heard about her myself,' she said. 'She used to run after Alexis shamelessly. She was a couple of years older than he was, I recall, and when his father actually married her, he must have despised them both.'

'I think he did,' said Karen quietly. 'So when this anniversary dinner party came up, I had to go, you see. I didn't want you to read some sordid story about me in the press.'

'But why didn't you tell us?' exclaimed her mother.

'Would you have understood?' Karen looked at them both.

Her father heaved a sigh, taking out his pipe and putting it between his teeth. 'I don't know,' he said. 'I suppose after the way I've gone on about Whitney, it was only natural that you should keep any mention of him out of this house.'

Karen bent her head. 'He's not like you said, you know,' she said, pleating the folds of the dressing-gown. 'I really think he's interested in the mill. He wants to make a success of it. Whatever else there is to say about him, he's not a layabout.'

Her father sniffed. 'No, well, perhaps not,' he conceded. 'But I'm a bit old to be taught new tricks.'

'Is that what he said?'

'No. I said it.' Her father turned away. 'But go on. You were telling us about the four of you going down to Howard Whitney's for the week-end.'

'Yes.' Karen cupped her face in her hands. 'All right. Well, we went, as you know. I was introduced to Alexis's father as his fiancée, as planned, and – and as he said you didn't know anything about it, his father agreed to keep it confidential – for the time being.'

'I see.' Her father nodded. 'Just out of interest, how did old Howard take it?'

Karen shrugged. 'That was the amazing thing – he was delighted. He said – he said – oh, well, that's not important.' She flushed, and looked down at her hands. 'Then last night, at the dance which followed the dinner party, Michelle got drunk. Half-way through the proceedings, she got up on the dais and told the company that Alexis and I were going to be married.'

'She let the cat out of the bag,' said her mother dryly.

'Yes. But on purpose, I'm sure. She – she wanted to get back at us – for – for thwarting her.'

'But what if it had been the truth?' exclaimed her father.

Karen made a moue with her lips. 'Was it likely, I ask you? Much maligned though he may be, I can't see Alexis Whitney settling for someone like me.'

'Why not?' Her father was indignant.

'Oh, Pop, you know why not!' Karen hunched her

shoulders. 'So there you are. That's why I came away. I wanted nothing more to do with any of them.'

Laura shook her head. 'But what did he say afterwards? What did Ray say?'

Karen shuddered. 'Ray and I are through.'

Now her father took his pipe out of his mouth and stared at her incredulously. 'What?'

'Ray and I are through,' repeated Karen firmly. 'We – I – that is – it was a mistake. Our going together. It would never have worked.'

'But you were so close!' exclaimed her mother.

'We were friends, that was all,' said Karen, with a sigh. 'Just good friends. At last I understand the meaning of that phrase.'

'Well, I don't know.' Her father looked properly put out now. 'You go away for a week-end to enjoy yourself, and you come back on your own soaked to the skin, apparently out of friends with everybody.'

Karen managed a faint smile. 'Oh, Pop, you make it sound so – so ridiculous somehow.'

'Well, it is ridiculous!' retorted her father flatly. 'Good heavens, you and Ray have known one another for years. You can't just decide overnight that you don't care for him any more.'

'I haven't decided overnight, as you put it. I've known for ages really. I just haven't wanted to commit myself. Pop, if I'd wanted to marry Ray, we'd have got engaged ages ago.'

'That's true,' her mother nodded sagely. 'I told her she was a fool the other day when she refused to talk seriously about marriage. But I'm sorry all the same. Ray's a nice boy.'

'Yes.' Karen suddenly felt unutterably tired. The sleepless night she had experienced, the soaking and the hot bath, and now the heat of the fire were all combining to draw the strength out of her. 'Oh, Mum,' she said, 'would you mind if I went to bed? I feel exhausted.'

Laura looked at her husband for confirmation and then back at Karen. 'If that's what you'd like to do, of course,' she said. 'Do you want anything to eat?'

'Not right now,' said Karen, getting to her feet. 'I'll come down later. If I can just have a couple of hours . . .'

But in fact, Karen had many more than a couple of hours. She was sound asleep when the doorbell of the small house rang just after five o'clock, and when Laura went to answer it she found Alexis Whitney on the doorstep, beads of water standing on the thick, water-darkened smoothness of his hair.

'Is Karen here?'

His first words were abrupt, and Laura found herself nodding, and saying: 'Yes. Yes, she's here. She arrived home about two hours ago.'

'Can I see her?' Alexis's jaw was tight, and a muscle was jerking low on his cheekbone.

'I'm afraid not.' Laura was firm. 'She's asleep at the moment, and I don't want to disturb her.'

Alexis dragged up the collar of his suède jacket about his ears as rain trickled down his neck from his wet hair. 'Do you think she'll sleep long?' he asked. 'Could I perhaps wait and speak to her?'

Karen's father came into the hall. 'Who is it, Laura?' he asked, and then halted. 'Oh – it's you!'

'Yes.' Alexis looked resignedly as though he was prepared for a tirade which never came. 'I wanted to speak to Karen.'

'So I gather.' Daniel Sinclair glanced at his wife. 'Do you want to come in? Karen's in bed.'

Alexis was taken aback by the tolerance in Daniel Sinclair's tone. 'I'd like to come in very much,' he said.

Laura stood aside and he entered the narrow hallway, as before dwarfing it with his presence. In the living-room, Daniel took his coat and indicated that he should take a chair.

'You've just driven up from Maidenhead, I suppose.'

Alexis frowned, and looked questioningly at Laura. 'We know,' she said heavily. 'Karen told me where she was going before she left.'

'I see.' Alexis inclined his head, sitting on the couch, legs apart, his hands hanging loosely between.

'Would you like some tea?' Laura felt *de trop*.

Alexis shook his head. 'No, thank you.'

'Something stronger, perhaps?' Daniel rose to his feet again. 'Scotch?'

Alexis nodded. 'That would be fine.'

Daniel poured two drinks and handed one to Alexis while Laura excused herself on the pretext of seeing to some cakes she had in the oven. The two men sat for a while in silence, enjoying the Scotch, and then Daniel said: 'Filthy weather.'

Alexis dragged his thoughts back to the present with obvious difficulty. 'Yes,' he said. 'Bad for driving.'

'Very bad,' Daniel nodded, lighting his pipe again. 'I see Leeds won yesterday.'

'Did they? I'm afraid I'm not familiar with soccer.'

'You're not?' Daniel was scandalized. 'And you a York-shireman!'

'I used to play rugby,' remarked Alexis mildly.

'Huh!' Daniel chewed at his pipe. 'There's no game like football.'

Alexis finished his drink. Then, studying the empty glass, he said: 'Look, suppose we cut the small talk. Exactly what did Karen tell you when she got back?'

Daniel frowned. 'What's it to you?'

Alexis sighed. 'She was upset, I realize that—'

'She was also soaked to the skin. She had to get out of the train at Leeds and make her own way here, and it was pouring down. Still is, by the looks of things.'

Alexis nodded, running a hand round the back of his neck. 'What a mess!' he muttered.

'Have you brought Ray and that lass back with you?'

'Shirley? Yes. I dropped them before coming on here.'

Daniel digested this. 'Bit of a fiasco, if you ask me. Karen should have told us the truth all along, and then none of this would have happened.'

Alexis regarded him sardonically. 'I doubt you would have shown the equanimity you're showing at the moment.'

'Perhaps not, perhaps not.' Daniel had to concede that. 'Anyway, what do you want to see her for? Surely you've done enough, taking her down there!'

Alexis rose to his feet. 'I have to talk to her,' he said.

'What about?'

'I want to explain—'

'Explain? Explain what? That that stepmother of yours is a bitch?'

Alexis turned away, and just then Laura came back into the room. 'What's going on, Dan?'

Alexis stood his empty glass on the mantelpiece. 'Is Karen still sleeping?'

'Yes. I've just been up to her. Poor kid, she's exhausted!'

'Yes. I'm sorry.' Alexis thrust his hands into his pockets. 'I suppose it would be best if I came back to see her tomorrow evening.'

'It would be best.'

'All right.' He walked to the door. 'Good night, then. Good night, Dan.'

'Good night.' Daniel rose to his feet and nodded farewell.

Laura saw him out and after he had gone she came back to the living-room. 'I wonder why he came,' she mused.

'To see that Karen was home safely.'

'Yes, but why did he want to talk to her?'

'I don't know. Anyway, it's not worth bothering about. Now, what about tea?'

Karen's wish that she might not have to face Ray and Shirley was realized in a way she had least expected.

The following morning, she awoke with a fuzzy head and a temperature that soared by the minute, and after taking one look at her Laura called the doctor. He came soon after ten and pronounced that Karen had caught a chill, and insisted that she stayed in bed.

Karen herself was quite content to comply. She felt pretty awful, and terribly weak. She slept almost the whole day, and by evening her cheeks were flushed and unhealthy.

Towards teatime her mother came to tell her that Ray had called to see her, but Karen shook her head vigorously, causing a veritable hammer to pound away in her temples, and declared that she didn't want to see anyone.

Laura didn't argue, and Ray went away again, but Laura realized she would have to tell her daughter that Alexis Whitney had called the previous evening, and that he, too, was likely to call again later.

'I don't want to see him,' said Karen throatily. 'I couldn't. Not right now. Wait until I'm feeling a bit more able to cope. Besides – besides, I look such a mess!'

Oh, Karen, what does that matter? What shall I tell him?'

'Tell him I'm asleep.'

'Not again.'

'Please, Mum. I couldn't face – I couldn't face him.'

Tears of weakness were gathering in her eyes, so Laura made no further effort to get her to change her mind, but Alexis was a different proposition from Ray.

'Is she awake?' he demanded harshly, when Laura said that Karen wasn't receiving visitors.

'Well, yes—'

'Then I'm going to see her.'

He put Laura firmly aside, and before she could stop

him he was half-way up the stairs. It was still daylight, and Daniel wasn't yet home from work, and she didn't know what to do. She made as though to follow him, but he halted at the top of the stairs and said: 'Please. Give me five minutes.'

With a sigh she turned away, and Alexis thrust open Karen's door and entered the room.

Karen had heard this interchange from a drowsy state of inertia which was banished by the vitality of his physical dominance. She put up an unsteady hand to her tousled hair, and said: 'What do you want?'

Alexis came to the bed, and looked down at her. 'Our positions are reversed,' he remarked, with some satisfaction.

'I told my mother I didn't want to see anybody.'

'I know. But I wanted to see you.'

'What makes you so special?' Karen drew the covers up to her nose.

'I wanted to talk to you.' He sat down on the side of the bed. 'Why did you run away yesterday?'

'I didn't run away. I *came* away. That's a different thing.'

'So – why did you come away? What were you afraid of?'

'I wasn't afraid of anything.' Karen turned her face into the pillow. 'I just didn't want anything more to do with it.'

'With me, you mean?' Alexis's eyes were hard.

'All right. With you, then.'

Alexis heaved a sigh. 'Why? I wasn't to blame for what Michelle said. Besides, as it happens there was no harm done. The only press who touched the story was a local rag, and even they played it down.'

'How nice for you! What a relief that must have been. I could have been suing you for breach of promise!'

'Karen!' He spoke her name savagely.

'Well? Isn't it true?' Karen moved her legs restlessly

177

under the bedcoverings. 'Anyway, it's all over now. I've told my parents the truth.'

'So I hear.'

'You won't be able to blackmail me any more—'

'I didn't blackmail you,' he snapped angrily.

'Didn't you? Well, somebody did.'

'Karen!' He rose abruptly to his feet. 'It's impossible to talk with you in this mood.'

'I'm sorry. But I did ask you not to come.'

'When do you think you'll be up and about again?'

'Why?'

'I want to see you.'

'Oh, no.'

'Karen, stop it!' His voice was rough. 'I *have* to see you again, damn you, and I don't care what anyone says!'

'Mr. Whitney!' Laura's voice came from the doorway. 'Is that any way to speak to a sick girl?'

Alexis turned abruptly. 'No, I guess it's not,' he muttered, and brushing past her he went out of the bedroom. They heard his footsteps on the stairs and then the hollow bang as the front door closed behind him.

In fact, Karen was not up and about again in a week as her parents and the doctor had expected her to be. In spite of their care and the use of antibiotics, the chill degenerated into pneumonia and for several days she was scarcely conscious of what was going on around her. Her temperature soared to a hundred and five and she felt so ill she almost wanted to die. But then the crisis came, and it broke leaving her weak but recovering. Even so, it was obvious it was going to be several weeks before she was completely well again.

Easter was approaching, and the weather was unseasonably mild after the harsh winter they had just experienced, and Laura suggested that Karen might go and spend a couple of weeks with her aunt in Keswick.

Karen had to smile at this, although in recent weeks

she seemed to have found little to smile about. But those wishes she had made on the bus had all come true, and she realized that it was possible to achieve something one had hoped for without the appreciation one had expected to feel. Right now, if she had been fit enough, she would have liked to have gone back to work. The activity would have acted as a kind of therapy, destroying the depressive state she seemed to have allowed herself to sink into. The doctor said it was natural, he said that it was a normal aftermath of a serious illness such as she had had, but she knew it wasn't so. At least not altogether. It had more to do with the fact that Alexis had not come back . . .

Ray had come to see her when she was first over the crisis. But they had been stilted with one another, both aware of what had happened that week-end at Falcons, but neither of them wishing to actually broach the subject. In consequence, he had not come back either, and she had not even had news of the school to buoy her failing confidence.

'Well?' her mother was saying now, as they sat together in the living-room one sunny afternoon. 'Do you think you'd like a couple of weeks away? I mean, you won't be able to return to school until after the Easter holidays, and a break might do you good.'

'All right.' Karen sounded listless.

'You might be a bit more enthusiastic about it,' remarked her mother dryly.

'I am, really. It's just that – well, you know the doctor said it would take time . . .'

And so, a few days later, Karen went to Keswick, to her Aunt Margaret's, in the hope that her mother's sister might effect the cure she had effected seven years before.

It was April now, and there were lambs in the fields, and the Lake District was wrapped in the wonderful aura of spring. Daffodils and wild narcissi grew in profusion at the lakeside, and already there were tourists poking

179

about in the gift and souvenir shops. Easter was always a busy time there and this particular Easter was no exception. Karen's parents came over to Keswick for a couple of days during the break and they all went out in the car touring the beauty spots.

To Karen's relief, her cousin Bryan, who had previously made quite a nuisance of himself where she was concerned, was now going out with a girl whose father farmed just outside of town, which meant that Karen was able to go about alone without arousing too much comment.

After her parents' return, her father wrote to her a couple of times. In one of his letters he mentioned that the assessment of Alexis's idea of the forklift truck had been made and plans were going ahead to dismantle the conveyor belt.

Although I was against the idea in the first instance, he wrote, *I find myself agreeing with him now. The conveyor belt was a slow-moving vehicle, at best, and it's much quicker and easier for one man to pick up a couple of bales and deposit them where one wants them. I don't think I quite understood the idea at first, but now I do. Things are quite amenable between us these days, and every week we have conferences to discuss ideas and manpower situations. This also was Alexis's idea, and I'm all for it.*

Karen finished the letter and folded it thoughtfully. So it was *Alexis* now, not that man Whitney! She sighed, and tried not to feel envious. If only her father had been like this in the early days, perhaps things might not have worked out as they did.

But such thoughts were futile, and she knew it. No matter what happened at the mill, she was still the submanager's daughter, and he was the son of the owner.

The comprehensive school was due to open two weeks after Easter, and Karen returned home one Thursday afternoon, four days before that event. She needed the week-end to catch up on her work, and she rang the head-master as soon as she got home to make arrangements to see her substitute. She was thinner than she had been before she went away, but at least she had lost that terribly fragile look, and her skin had assumed a warmer glow. The hollows beneath her eyes could not be disguised, however; they were due to the fact that she was sleeping badly, and Laura was most concerned about her.

'I'm sure you're not well enough to take up teaching!' she exclaimed, at once.

'The doctor says I'm physically fit,' returned Karen quietly. 'Time and work will make me well again, not wasting my time doing nothing.'

Laura sighed. 'Well, I don't agree, and I shall tell that doctor so when I see him.'

On Sunday, the day before school was due to open, Karen's parents announced that they were going out for the day.

'But where?' asked Karen in surprise. She was still in her dressing-gown, sitting at the table drinking her morning cup of coffee.

'I thought we might go to Scarborough,' said her father thoughtfully. 'Do you want to come?'

'You know I can't,' exclaimed Karen crossly. 'I told you last night I had lessons to prepare for tomorrow.'

'So you did.' Her father looked regretful. 'Well, never mind – you can come with us some other time.'

Karen rested her elbows on the kitchen table, cradling the cup in her hands. 'But what about lunch?' She looked at her mother. 'Is there a joint of meat to cook? Do you want me to make you a meal for when you come home?'

'Heavens, no!' Her mother shook her head. 'You just take it easy. We'll have our lunch out. If you make yourself a snack, we can have a proper meal when I get back.'

Karen shrugged. 'All right.'

But she was disappointed, and they knew it. This was her first Sunday at home for more than three weeks, and before that she had been too ill to care. It seemed mean of them to go off and leave her; but then she chided herself. Why shouldn't they, after all? Her problems weren't their problems, and just because she was feeling sorry for herself it didn't mean that they had to put themselves out to look after her ...

They drove away cheerfully, waving to her as she stood by the door, and then she went back inside and switched on the radio, and tried to tell herself that she would work better without anyone's interruption.

She was washing up her coffee cup at the sink before going to get dressed, when the doorbell rang. Sighing, she looked down at her appearance. Whoever could be calling at ten-thirty on a Sunday morning? It could only be Lucy from down the street, her mother's friend.

But when she opened the door, she stepped back aghast. Alexis Whitney was leaning negligently against the canopy support, looking lean and attractive in a navy canvas suit with a navy shirt to match. His tawny eyes flickered over her with disturbing appraisal, making her overwhelmingly aware of the limitations of her quilted dressing-gown, and the tangled darkness of her hair. Then he said, 'Hello, Karen. Can I come in?'

Karen shook her head slowly, gathering her composure with difficulty. 'My – my father's not here. He – he's gone out for the day – with – with my mother.'

'I know that. I saw them leave,' remarked Alexis lazily, and stepped into the hall, taking the door from her unresisting fingers and closing it behind him.

Karen swallowed with difficulty. 'I don't know what you think you're doing—' she began, but the look in his eyes silenced her.

'I know exactly what I'm doing,' he replied, with emphasis. 'Now – can we go into the living-room?'

Karen made a helpless movement of her shoulders. His unexpected appearance had unnerved her, and she began to appreciate how weak she still was. It actually took a tremendous effort of will power not to make some movement towards him, to touch him, to assure herself that she wasn't having hallucinations on top of everything else.

Turning, she led the way into the living-room, automatically bending to pick up a newspaper lying on a chair, to straighten a cushion on the couch. Alexis followed her, tall and disruptive, his presence as always a threat to her peace of mind.

'If – if you'll excuse me a moment, I'll go and put on some clothes,' she murmured awkwardly, but he shook his head.

'Don't bother. I like you as you are.'

'Maybe you do, but there are neighbours—'

'I don't particularly care what your neighbours think,' remarked Alexis, his eyes holding hers. 'You're very nervous, Karen. Why?'

'I – I haven't been well—'

'No, that's obvious. You've lost weight. How are you feeling now?'

'I'm fine.' Karen drew a shaking breath. 'I'm going back to work tomorrow.'

'You look very pale,' said Alexis, standing, feet apart, his arms folded, regarding her. 'And you've dark rings round your eyes. I think you need a holiday, not the arduous duties of a teacher.'

Karen put up a hand to her hair almost defensively. 'I know I must look a mess—' she began.

'I didn't say that!'

'No, but you meant it,' Karen shrugged. 'Besides, I'm not wearing any make-up. It's amazing what make-up can do—'

Alexis shook his head impatiently. 'Oh, Karen, stop talking nonsense! You know perfectly well that I don't intend to let you go back to work tomorrow – or ever!'

and grasping her shoulders he pulled her towards him.

Karen's hands were crushed against his chest as he bent his head to hers, finding the warm, scented skin of her nape with his mouth. Her weakened senses betrayed her then. For so long she had wanted to be where she was now that the idea of resisting didn't come until later. The warmth and masculinity of him was all about her, the muscles of his thighs were hard against hers, and with a little groan she slid her arms round his waist and lifted her mouth to his.

The hungry weeks of wanting him, of needing him, of longing to touch him were over and coherent thought dissolved beneath the onslaught of his demands. She wanted to give and give, and although she pressed herself against him it was not close enough. She wanted to be a part of him.

But then he moved, his hands reaching her forearms, dragging them from around him, and pressing her firmly away from him. He was breathing rather heavily and the tawny eyes were slightly glazed. Only then did Karen realize what she had been doing, how wantonly she had behaved, offering herself to him without thought of denial, seduced by her own desires into complete surrender.

'Karen,' he began hoarsely, when she wrenched herself away from him, turning her back.

'Don't say anything!' she cried, pressing her balled fists to her lips. 'Just – just go!'

'Karen!' he said again, and this time there was torment in his voice. 'Karen, don't be a fool! I had to push you away, or God help me I'd have been unable to do so! Don't you know what you've done to me?'

Karen was finding it difficult to breathe at all. 'What – what are you trying to say?'

Alexis uttered a muffled imprecation and then slid his arms around her from behind, hauling her back against him, holding her there as though he couldn't bear to let her go. 'You know I want you,' he said huskily, his hands probing between the lapels of her dressing-gown. 'What you don't seem to be aware of is that I love you. And love is not a word I've used to any woman before.'

Karen's body relaxed against his. 'You – love – me,' she breathed incredulously.

'Yes. I love you.' Alexis bent his head and kissed the side of her neck. 'And holding you like this is killing when I know I can't make love to you.'

Karen tried to think. Resting her head back against his chest, she said tremulously: 'Why can't you?'

Now Alexis propelled her away from him again, and she turned to face him in surprise. He took a step backward and dropped down on to the couch, stretching his long legs out before him in an attitude of complete abandon.

'Oh, Karen,' he said, shaking his head from side to side. 'Do you know what you're saying?'

Karen pressed the palms of her hands to her cheeks to hide their burning. 'Yes, I know,' she said.

Alexis's eyes narrowed. 'And you've never said that to anyone else before, have you?'

'No!' She was indignant.

'Good.' He half smiled. 'Now – make me some coffee while I try to think of other things.'

'What – other things?' Karen was perplexed.

'Well, this, for one.' Alexis drew a document out of his inside pocket and handed it to her. 'Go on, read it.'

Karen opened it slowly and then looked up in astonishment. 'It – it's a marriage licence!' she murmured faintly.

'Not *a* marriage licence – *our* marriage licence,' remarked Alexis quietly.

'Ours?' Karen stared down at the paper in her hand. 'But – but you haven't asked me to marry you!'

'Do I have to do that?' Alexis was ironic.

Karen made a helpless gesture. 'I – I don't know.'

'All right. If that's what you want.' He swung himself off the couch and knelt before her on one knee, taking her hand and raising it to his lips. 'Karen, darling Karen, will you marry me?'

Karen nodded, looking down at him wonderingly, and suddenly his hands gripped her hips, drawing her down beside him, his mouth finding hers, imprisoning it, bearing her back against the hearthrug with passionate intensity.

'Karen, Karen, Karen,' he groaned, burying his face in the hollow of her neck. 'I've loved you since the day you tumbled down the mountain and into that snowdrift. I haven't been able to think of another woman since then, let alone make love to one. You're under my skin, you disturb my nights, you haunt my days; I don't think I could live without you now.'

Karen stroked the hair back from his forehead and tried to believe this was really happening. 'But – but – you seemed to dislike me. Whenever we were together—'

'Whenever we were together, I had Nichols rammed down my throat,' said Alexis fiercely. 'He was your boy-friend, you'd known each other for years, you were going to marry him, while I—' he shook his head, 'I wasn't even welcome in your house.'

Karen looked up at him lovingly. 'But, Alexis, you're different from us. There's such a gulf between us. How could I take you seriously?'

'You're taking me seriously now, aren't you?' he demanded harshly, and she glimpsed the old arrogance he could display.

'Yes,' she said, touching his mouth with her fingers. 'But you've got to admit—'

'I admit nothing! How was there a gulf between us? I was born in Wakeley, just as you were. My father worked in the mill, just as your father does. The fact that my father made more money at it is purely coincidental.'

Karen smiled. 'You've had a very different life from me.'

'I should hope so, too,' he muttered, putting his lips to the hollow between her breasts. 'I want to teach you all there is to know about making love. I don't want anyone else to have touched you.'

Karen coloured lightly. 'That sounds rather Victorian.'

'Didn't you know? Reformed rakes make the most forbidding husbands?' he mocked her.

Karen frowned. 'You made such ridiculous reasons for seeing me. That trip to London, for example.'

Alexis sighed. 'That trip to London, as you put it, was a complete fiasco. I engineered it as an exercise where we might be together for forty-eight hours, and what happened? You brought Ray along, and that other girl.'

'You engineered it?' Karen echoed now. 'How do you mean?'

Alexis looked rather sheepish. 'You don't think I can't handle Michelle by now, do you?'

'You mean – you mean – you made it all up?' Karen stared at him.

'I'm sorry.' Alexis's lips curved into a smile.

'But – but at the dance – that announcement!'

'What of it? Everyone knows what Michelle is like. But as a matter of fact, I didn't rescind it.'

Karen propped herself up on her elbows. 'You mean – your father still thinks we're engaged?'

'Well, aren't we?' asked Alexis mockingly, and Karen sank back again helplessly.

Then another thought struck her. 'Today, when you came – you said you saw my parents leave. How did you know they were going out?'

'They told me. It was all arranged.'

'You mean – you mean – they know!'

'Well, let's say they know how *I* feel.' His eyes were amused and caressing.

Karen felt an overwhelming sense of happiness. 'You told them—'

'—that I wanted to marry you? Right.'

'And – and what did they say?'

Alexis shrugged. 'The usual things. Of course, there was one thing.'

'What?' Karen was vaguely apprehensive.

'Well, I had to explain that I had no intention of going back to London to live. That I intended keeping on with the job at the mill!'

'Oh, Alexis!' Karen caught her breath. 'Oh, Alexis, I do love you!'

'I thought it was about time you said that,' he remarked complacently. 'By the way, you know what you said about swimming in the Bahamas? Well, it just so happens that my father has a house there. I don't suppose you'd like to go there for our honeymoon, would you . . .'

Golden Harlequin $2.25 per vol.
Each Volume Contains 3 Complete Harlequin Romances

☐ ## Volume 20

DOCTOR SARA COMES HOME by Elizabeth Houghton (#594)
After an unfortunate mishap, Sara Lloyd, a brilliant doctor went to live for a year in the delightful but remote Welsh Mountains. Coming to terms with life again, she found Robert Llewellyn becoming a very dear friend, then, suddenly, out of her "hidden" past walked — Stephen Grey.

THE TALL PINES by Celine Conway (#736)
Bret was deeply involved in chemical research in Western Canada. The last thing he needed on his mind was this pale, fragile English girl, and her foolishly quixotic mission. The "last thing" soon became the most important part of his whole life . . .

ACROSS THE COUNTER by Mary Burchell (#603)
Katherine was assigned to re-organize one of Kendales' departments in the Midlands. Within a week, she became engaged to Paul Kendale while she still loved someone else — it wasn't the shop, but her own life which underwent the greatest change . . .

☐ ## Volume 21

THE DOCTOR'S DAUGHTERS by Anne Weale (#716)
When the new squire arrived at Dr. Burney's busy and pleasant household, his presence became a disturbing influence on the lives of all the doctor's family. It was the eldest daughter, Rachel, who quickly found that Daniel Elliot was not a man to be ignored:

GATES OF DAWN by Susan Barrie (#792)
Richard Trenchard was accustomed to having his own way, not least with women. This applied even to his sister, and to her secretary, Melanie Brooks, who fell victim to Richard's power. But, in the end, was it Richard, or Melanie, who really did have their way?

THE GIRL AT SNOWY RIVER by Joyce Dingwell (#808)
Upon arrival in Australia, Prudence found herself the only girl among 400 men! To most women, this would have been heavenly. But, what if the most important of these men is determined to get rid of you — as was precisely the case . . .

Golden Garlequin $2.25 per vol.
Each Volume Contains 3 Complete
Harlequin Romances

☐ Volume 25

DOCTOR MEMSAHIB by Juliet Shore   (#531)
Mark Travers had little use for a woman plastic surgeon in his
hospital in Bengal, but the Rajah had requested her, so he might
make use of her visit. An accusing, anonymous letter had
preceded Ruth's arrival, and try as he did, Mark could not quite
put it out of his head . . .

AND BE THY LOVE by Rose Burghley   (#617)
"Is it necessary to know all there is to know about a man or
woman before falling in love with him or her?" When Caroline was
asked this question, her answer came easily. It was later that she
would have cause to weigh the value of these words . . .

BLACK CHARLES by Esther Wyndham   (#680)
A man who would never marry! Whose character was arrogant and
fierce! He was the one dark haired male born of this generation
into the Pendleton family, and alas, it was the fate of young
Audrey Lawrence to cross swords with — Black Charles Pendleton.

☐ Volume 27

SANDFLOWER by Jane Arbor   (#576)
Both girls were named Elizabeth. Roger Yate thought Liz to be
forceful and courageous, and Beth, sweet appealing little Beth. In
his opinion of the characters of these two girls, the brilliant young
doctor could not have been more wrong!

NURSE TRENT'S CHILDREN by Joyce Dingwell   (#626)
A tragic accident had ended Cathy's training, so she came to
Australia as housemother to a number of orphaned children. Dr.
Jeremy Malcolm seemed to take an immediate dislike to her
organization, and more particularly, to Cathy herself.

INHERIT MY HEART by Mary Burchell   (#782)
The only way left for Mrs. Thurrock and her daughter Naomi to
share the inheritance now, was for Naomi to marry Jerome. It
might have been a good idea, if only Naomi hadn't infinitely
preferred his brother, Martin . . .

Golden Harlequin $2.25 per vol.
Each Volume Contains 3 Complete
Harlequin Romances

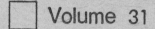 ## Volume 31

THE HOUSE ON FLAMINGO CAY by Anne Weale (#743)
Angela Gordon was glamorous and ambitious, and confident that
in the Bahamas she would find herself a rich husband. The
wealthy Stephen Rand was perfect, but alas — he was much more
attracted by her sister Sara's quieter charms . . .

THE WEDDING DRESS by Mary Burchell (#813)
Loraine could hardly contain herself, she was going from the
seclusion of an English boarding school, straight into the heady
atmosphere of Paris, in May. Her only concern was, her unknown
guardian — and his plans for her . . .

TOWARDS THE SUN by Rosalind Brett (#693)
There was a warm loveliness all around her on the sun-soaked
South Sea island of Bali, yet, Sherlie was miserable. She was
exploited by a chilly stepmother and even worse, she fell in love
with the totally inaccessible — Paul Stewart.

Volume 32

DOCTOR'S ASSISTANT by Celine Conway (#826)
Laurette decided that Charles Heron was an autocrat, who
thought far too much of himself. She also knew that she meant
absolutely nothing in his life — a suitable situation? Quite, —
until she realized, that for the very first time, she was in love!

TENDER CONQUEST by Joyce Dingwell (#854)
Bridget found her work fascinating. She loved travelling around,
meeting and talking to all sorts of people, who all seemed to
enjoy talking to her. All, except the new Market Research
Manager, who considered her quite inefficient.

WHEN YOU HAVE FOUND ME by Elizabeth Hoy (#526)
During the crossing to Ireland, Cathleen offered to take care of a
small kitten. A friendly gesture, which had some far reaching
consequences, leading her to some very strange — and exciting
results!